From Fire into Fire

An Isaac's House Novella

NORMANDIE FISCHER

From Fire
into
Fire

An Isaac's House Novella

NORMANDIE FISCHER

Sleepy Creek Press
Gloucester, NC

Copyright © 2016 by Normandie Fischer

All rights reserved. No part of this publication may be reproduced, distributed or transmitted in any form or by any means, including photocopying, recording, or other electronic or mechanical methods, without the prior written permission of the publisher, except in the case of brief quotations embodied in critical reviews and certain other noncommercial uses permitted by copyright law. For permission requests, write to the publisher.
Sleepy Creek Press
www.sleepycreekpress.com
Publisher's Note: This is a work of fiction. Names, characters, places, and incidents are a product of the author's imagination. Locales and public names are sometimes used for atmospheric purposes. Any resemblance to actual people, living or dead, or to businesses, companies, events, institutions, or locales is completely coincidental.

Cover Design by Jenny from Seedlings Design
From Fire into Fire/Normandie Fischer -- 1st ed.

*Dedicated to the warriors among us, especially my beloveds:
Michael,
Joshua, and Ariana*

1 MEIRA

"*Allahu Akbar!*"

The madman's cry flashed into memory, and Meira saw again the knife-wielder who'd proclaimed his god greater than all others. He'd pounced, his face so close to hers that his spittle had dripped down her cheek. But he'd missed his mark, and she, though scarred, had lived.

What she and David planned to do today brought into full relief all that had happened sixteen years ago, along with the fear that hearing their truth would leave indelible scars on their son.

Here in rural New York, gulls screeched over the placid lake, and the sun angled its way into day. She pressed her bare feet against the porch floorboards to set her rocker in motion and tried to get her pencil working to sketch something, anything. Maybe the scratch of lead on paper, the rhythmic creak of the old boards, and the back and forth, back and forth, would erase memories of the men—and the woman—who'd brandished those words along with a knife, a gun, and a bomb. Or maybe, if the memory glued itself to her thoughts like sticky tape, she could use it to help with what was to come.

Behind her, the cottage waited, cool and welcoming, their safety net in the early years and the place that had allowed them to pretend to be normal once they'd begun their undercover life as Arabs. Would it cocoon them as well after the tale was told? She prayed so.

She and David knew the difference between the truth and a lie. Knew it intimately. Moral relativism, that posh term for a decadent point of view, didn't fit either of them, and yet they lied for a living.

She stared out at the lake, where the light shimmered on the water, silhouetting David as he lowered himself to the dock next to their son. The sun, edging its way over the horizon, blurred images just as their lies had smeared the charcoal portrait of their life.

And now they were about to break into truth with the one who meant the world to them. It made her gut hurt, because Tony would hate them after this day's work. He'd think their truths putrid because of what the years in Lebanon had taught him.

He turned and waved his rod, obviously wanting her to remember his promise of fish for tonight. "Today I'll catch the big one, Mom. I can feel it. Today is my lucky day."

Tears had welled at the words, but he'd merely glanced at his dad and grinned. Her men often shared that look, the one that meant women were incomprehensible to the male mind.

FROM FIRE INTO FIRE

David and Tony baited their hooks and tossed lines off the dock's edge. She couldn't see the splash of the weight as it pulled the morsel down to fish level, but she could imagine it. Imagine the plop as it hit the water and her boy's grin because they were out there again, with the promise of dinner waiting to be reeled in.

If only fishing were all they had to do today. If only.

2 Tony

Tony braced his fishing rod against the dock, steadying it with one hand as he examined the bucket of wiggling earthworms. "You think those are good enough as bait?"

His dad nodded. "Good enough."

"That guy at the shop, he said he uses lures."

"We have some if these don't work, but the fish liked worms when I was a kid. Doubt they've changed preferences."

Tony bent to stare at the floating cork, waiting for anything that looked like a bite on his line. They'd only been here a couple of days, and his dad seemed kind of tense. Mom said they'd come home from Lebanon for a vacation, and a vacation was supposed to relax you, wasn't it? Maybe canoeing and catching fish would do the trick. Tony was determined to catch a good one before he left, bigger than legal, so maybe two feet. Wouldn't that be trophy sized? He grinned at the thought of the letter he'd send back to Bahir. With a picture. And he'd promised himself he'd swim all the way to the diving platform this year. Get his dad to take a picture of that, too.

They'd probably take a bunch of photos of that stupid boarding school they were forcing him to go to instead of letting him go back to Lebanon with them. Only because some stupid jerks had beat up on him and Bahir. He was fine. Or almost. His black eye had turned yellow, so that meant it was almost good as new, and the rest of him didn't hurt so bad anymore. He and Bahir'd just have to watch out and not go to the beach without other friends around. They could be careful.

But the school had said yes to taking him. So he guessed it was set—unless he could talk Mom and Dad out of it in the next couple of months.

He tugged at his shorts, which were kinda snug and kinda high up his leg. Maybe he was finally starting to grow. He sure didn't want to go to some dumb new school if he still looked like a kid. No one would believe he'd be fourteen his next birthday. He looked ten.

The other guys back in Beirut, like Bahir, were growing or were already big. Some had muscles, really good ones. Tony's arms still stuck out like sticks with lumps the size of lemons where he'd tried for biceps. His dad promised it wouldn't be long before he grew, but what did Dad know about long? When you were the puny one in a group, "not long" seemed like forever.

Poor Bahir was mad because he couldn't get rid of the kid pudge he'd carried for as long as Tony'd known him. It must be from his mother's side, because Bahir's dad was tall and real skinny. Or maybe Bahir just hadn't got there yet. All Tony wanted was to start catching up with his dad. Then maybe his voice would change, and he wouldn't feel like such a wimp. And no one would freak out when he and Bahir when alone to the beach. He liked Lebanon, especially with a best friend. The Mediterranean sure beat anything they had in New York.

He heard a plop out on the lake and looked down at his line, willing a fish to swim in this direction. "You think we should try one of those lures yet?" he asked.

"Give it time." Dad lifted and lowered his rod so his cork bobbed.

Tony sighed and went back to worrying that he might take after his mom. She was little, but at least her dad and her brother weren't. They lived in Israel. Tony didn't get why they'd want to be *there*. Plus, his grandmother sure cried a lot. Dad said that was just the way some women did things. Got weepy over movies and saying goodbye.

Anyway, until he grew some, he didn't think going away to school would work for him.

"This is great, isn't it?" Dad said. "Just the two of us."

"Yeah."

"I'm glad we're out here alone, because I need to talk to you."

Tony shifted position. "Okay."

Dad didn't say any more. Guys did silence. Tony got that, but not when one of them said he wanted to talk and the other agreed to listen.

Finally, his father cleared his throat. "It's about you, us, our family." He pulled at his line again, tweaking it like he wanted to check for a bite. "You know how you've always been with Arabic children and speak their language as well as you do English?"

Tony flattened himself on his stomach to look over the

edge of the dock. The dark water lapped against the pilings. Sometimes it sounded like a burp. "Sure," he said.

"You remember that your grandfather's father was Armenian and where Armenia is?"

"Sure."

"What you may not know is that he was a Christian whose family fled genocide in 1917 and moved to Israel. He lived and traded with the Jews and the Arabs there. Then one day he fell in love with your great-grandmother."

"We've got a picture of her. She was beautiful."

"Yes, she was beautiful. And great-granddaddy Yerev loved her and wanted to marry her, but her father thought it was a terrible thing. Yerev's family and friends weren't any happier."

Something in the way his father spoke made him sit up again. He didn't like the look on his dad's face, like right before Tony got in trouble. Only, this wasn't the mad voice.

His father said, "Your great-grandmother was..." and swallowed a word. Then it came out whole. "Miriam was a Jew."

Jew? Tony took a moment to make sure that's what he'd heard. "Jew? No way."

"Yes, she was."

"You mean like the Israelis?"

"She was an Israeli Jew." His dad put down his fishing rod.

Tony stared out over the water. He picked out one lonely cloud, like a rhino's head with its horn. "How can my grandmother be a Jew and me be an Arab? Did she change?"

"Well, son, that's what I'm trying to tell you. I guess it boils down to you not being an Arab."

Wait. That couldn't be true. He was an Arab. They were all Arabs. They didn't worship some Jewish God. Because Arabs didn't.

"My grandfather Yerev figured the God of the Christian and the God of the Jew were the same, so it didn't much matter that Miriam wanted to raise my father a Jew. Both of my parents were Americans, but they were born in Israel."

Tony could barely squeak out his next question. "What about Mom?"

"Jewish."

No. No way.

He swallowed back the saliva that started to fill his mouth. This didn't make any sense at all. If what Dad said was true, that meant . . . they'd lied. His whole family was a bunch of liars.

"We wanted to tell you from the beginning, but for your safety we've let you think we were all Arab-Americans. If you had known the truth, it would have been dangerous for you."

"But . . . why?"

"I think you know why."

"You lied." That was all that mattered. "All my life." He scrambled to his feet, his fists brushing his sides.

"Son."

"No. Just no."

"We didn't lie," his father said as Tony turned toward the house. "We just didn't tell you the whole truth."

"And that's not lying?" He spoke the words that came to him, the emotion that choked him. "I . . . I hate you."

The build-up of saliva had become bile as his stomach knotted and threatened to punch his breakfast up and out, and he crouched, just in case.

3   Tony

He was going to puke right here, right in front of his now-silent father, the man he'd believed in, trusted. Until this moment. Until his dad had pronounced this . . . what was the word for it? This *blasphemy*. Bahir's tutor had told them what shouldn't be said or even imagined. What would anger Allah. How Allah hated Jews.

Dad's words made *him* a Jew, too, didn't they? But he couldn't be one. His friends were Arabs. They used to spit the word *Jew* like a glob of gunk on the hard ground as the term took wing among them. He and Bahir and some of the other guys were going to be part of taking back Israel for the Palestinians. For Bahir's family.

He'd been right there with them. Proud, like the others, with his still-skinny chest sticking out and his fists pumping the air—against Israel.

He dashed down the dock as fast as his shrimpy legs would carry him. Back to the cabin, straight past his mother, the other liar. He went to the bathroom, slammed the door, and threw up all his breakfast.

His mother finally pushed her way in. He was sitting on the tile floor, his knees up, his head resting on his folded arms.

"Tony, honey."

He didn't raise his head. "Don't."

"Oh, Tony. Oh, my darling." His mother sat on the cold floor beside him. He stiffened, because no way was she going to get all lovey-dovey with him now he knew the truth.

He kept his head down. "All my life. You've lied to me. All. My. Life."

"I'm so . . . so sorry, so very sorry." Tears messed up her words until they came out on a sniffle. "We never wanted to leave you out of things, but it was the only way to keep you safe. We love you so much, my darling boy." She smoothed his hair.

He jerked away. Her hand felt wrong. It wasn't his real mother's hand.

"Why?" He sounded like a weakling. He cleared his throat. He would not be weak. "Why'd you do it? Pretend all these years?"

His father pushed the door the rest of the way open, his sandaled feet stopping close enough for Tony to see the hairs sticking out the top of his toes.

"Come out here, both of you," Dad said, "and we'll try to explain." He helped Mom up.

Tony took a minute more. He didn't want to follow. He didn't want to do anything they said, ever again, but he needed answers. In the living room, he flung himself down on the big leather couch, but then Mom sat in the middle, and he had to scoot over more. He should have picked a chair instead, because now they were lined up like one happy family.

"Just listen and try not to judge until you've heard it all. Can you do that?" Dad angled so he faced them both.

Maybe they figured they'd sit next to each other so they could gang up against him. Tony stared at the floor. He'd have to answer sooner or later. If he didn't, his dad would wait forever, just to make him squirm. So, he nodded.

"Your grandfather's full name was Anthony Rassadim. I was born David Rassadim. You were named after my father."

Tony groaned.

"You said you'd listen."

He started chewing the inside of his cheek. It was that or run.

"Our family can trace its lineage for hundreds and hundreds of years," Dad said, "and God has been with us all through that time."

Mom took Dad's hand. Solidarity, that's what they were after. Well, that was obviously nothing new. Leaving him out meant they'd been solidly against him from the beginning.

"Your other grandmother, the one you know," Dad continued, "lost all her family in Hitler's Germany, in gas chambers during the Holocaust."

Maybe that's why she cried so much. Or maybe she cried because she lied, too. "Some of the guys say the Holocaust didn't happen, that it's only a lie the Jews tell."

"It was very real to my mother," Mom said, "and to the six million who died at Hitler's hand. Ima knew what it meant to suffer and fear, to go hungry and watch people die, to wonder always if there would ever be a place where a Jew would be welcome. And then there was Israel."

He opened his mouth to speak again, but his father stopped him. "Don't say anything yet. Listen to what we tell you. Then you may speak."

He couldn't look at them, so he stared down at his hands. He expected to see claws or something awful now he knew these were Jewish hands.

4 MEIRA

She'd known this would be hard, but nothing could have prepared her for the reality of it. Her boy, so wounded, sitting there with slumped shoulders. So distant.

Thirteen was a vulnerable age, half boy and half man. Maybe they should have done this sooner. Or quit their undercover life before it became an issue.

Or never agreed to do it at all.

They'd sheltered him from the brutality of militant terrorist warfare. All he'd known were the angry words, not the senseless slaughter or the suicide bombers—except perhaps in the abstract. Never in terms of innocents dying.

She leaned toward him slightly, longing to bridge a gap that seemed much wider than the mere twelve inches separating them. The couch seemed bigger suddenly, the leather colder with an invisible barrier lowered between them, blocking touch. All she had were words.

And so she used them. "I met your father in 1979, in Jerusalem. I can still picture the scene as if it were yesterday. I'd just left the art school at the end of the day. The school secretary, Rachel, called a goodbye, and I turned to answer. I'd gone about a hundred yards toward Ben Yehuda Street and the intersection where I could catch a bus when a black *hajib* caught my attention."

Tony stirred and asked, "A *hajib*? Is that one of those veil things some of the women wear in Beirut?"

"I know the names are confusing, but you're thinking of the *niqab*, which hides all but a woman's eyes. The *hajib* is tied around the head to hide the hair but to accentuate the face." She smiled, but his expression sobered her immediately. She struggled to form the next words. "So . . . anyway, this Arab's scarf hung differently from the way it's designed to be tied. It draped low over the forehead, hiding her face as she focused her attention on the sidewalk. I wondered if she were worried about stepping in camel dung or dog droppings as she climbed from the car."

"As if there'd been camels anywhere near the streets of Jerusalem for decades," David said, trying to add a dose of humor.

She appreciated his effort. "Yes, well, the thing was, this woman wasn't actually a woman, but a man trying to hide in women's garb. I got a look at her—I mean his—face after he dropped a package in the rubbish bin. He turned in my direction, keeping his head low until he was almost in front of me and then he looked up, right into my eyes. I suppose he didn't stop to deal with me because he wanted to put as much distance as possible between himself and that trash bin, but he saw me—and I saw him. That's when the trouble began."

∽

1979

Just like that, the certainty of what was about to happen slammed into Meira, but she turned when she should have called for help, stared at his retreating form when she should have fled.

She tried to corral her thoughts into action as she looked again at the bin, but the force of the blast knocked her over, and she hit the pavement hard, landing on her art satchel. As she attempted to cover her face and turn away, the pain in her skull, in her leg, now in her back, crippled her. Her ears rang. Screams, wails, all sounded muffled.

That man had planted a bomb, and the something everyone in Jerusalem, in all of Israel, prayed would never come this close, had come close enough to kill. Not her this time. But others must be dead, maimed. She had to help. Someone had to help.

Dust and smoke almost overwhelmed the dark, coppery scent of blood that trickled across her cheek to her lips. Or maybe it was the metallic taste in her mouth that made her think of copper. She imagined destruction out there. The area around the bin would be chaos. There'd be bodies sprawled, limbs torn. Eyes staring blindly.

She swallowed a scream that would be less than useless as the air filled with sirens and weeping, cries of anguish. Words broke through the ringing in her ears. She caught the sound of Arabic and French, but the pleas for mercy were almost exclusively in her native Hebrew. She whispered a prayer that no one had died. That she wouldn't die. And although others probably had, she didn't imagine she would. Not today.

Feet, the slap of sandals, passed nearby, along with the pounding of heavier shoes. She should stand and run, shouldn't she, at least to help? But she couldn't move.

And then something tripped and fell on her, a body, warm flesh, filthy and stinking of sweat, maybe of urine. There was a cry, hers, she thought, and a moan, before the body rolled to the side and pushed itself up, cursing, as it—he—fled.

She should flee, too, if for no other reason than to keep from being trampled, but knives sliced through her leg when she moved it even slightly. "Adonai, have mercy," she whispered.

And then a hand clasped her arm. Someone said, "Come," in Hebrew. Said it gently. Said it close to her ear. "Let me help you."

She gazed up into eyes that were a dark blue, surprisingly gentle as they stared back. The hair was brown under its covering of dust. "My leg." Her throat had clogged. She cleared it.

"Which one?" he asked, swiping blood off his forehead from a cut just below his hairline.

She wore trousers, loose ones for comfort. "The right. It may be bleeding on the back side."

"Do you think it's broken? Is it the thigh or the calf?" He spoke with an accent. American?

"Below the knee. Not broken. Cut, I imagine. I twisted it, but this feels like a gash. Maybe from something in my art bag." She hoped that's what it was. "But you should help the others. I will be fine."

"No," he said in that calm, reasonable tone that provided such comfort. "There is help enough for the other wounded. I'll get you home."

FROM FIRE INTO FIRE

"Perhaps you could just call my father? He will come." And this man would know she had protection, the protection of a father. Because who was he, this would-be rescuer? He could be a friend of that Arab, come to finish the job.

She closed her eyes. No, that was absurd. He'd also been hit by debris. Besides, he was American.

"Your father won't be allowed through. I am here. Let me."

He scooped her up, along with her bag, cradling her like a baby against his chest, one strong arm under her knees. She moaned. She tried not to, but knives shot through her leg when it dangled like that. She was probably bleeding all over him.

"I'm so sorry," he said. "Perhaps I should take you to the hospital first."

"No. The hospital will be packed with people in worse shape."

"Then we'll get to my car, and you can tell me where to go."

He took care as he walked, as if she were a precious burden. No one had carried her since she was a child, and although her father's arms often held her, this stranger's care felt overwhelming in ways that left her breathless. Under the coating of dust and the stench of smoke, she could detect the slight odor of something else, something male that set her heart to *thurumping* in a way that had nothing to do with adrenaline and fear.

Tony brought her back to the present. "Mom . . . gagging here." He pointed his finger into his mouth and made a retching sound.

She hated that gesture. Instead of dealing with it, she said, "Oh, right. Sorry." Only, she wasn't sorry. It wouldn't hurt her boy to know how she'd felt about his father from the first moment of meeting him, of him touching her.

"How do you know it was an Arab and not a Jew being sneaky? That's what they do." Tony rubbed his forearms.

She reached out to cover the hand nearest her. "Honey, are you cold?" When he shook his head and drew away, she asked, "Then tell me, why would a Jew have planted a bomb that killed all those other Jews?"

"By accident?"

"No. He picked a busy street corner where mostly Jews shopped. There wasn't a single Arab killed."

"Besides," David said, "the next afternoon, the PFLP, the Popular Front for the Liberation of Palestine, claimed responsibility for setting it."

"Yeah, right." Tony crossed his arms. A scowl dragged his lips into a line. "That was probably made up, too. Like the rest."

Her husband's expression hardened in response. "I'm willing to be patient, young man, but you're pushing the limits with that attitude. You need to listen and use the brain you've been given."

The pout grew, and Tony's eventual "Sorry" sounded more sullen than apologetic.

"I want you to picture the street right after the bombing," David said.

"I thought you were going to talk about afterward."

"We will. But I want you to see the thing from my perspective. I was only a tourist in Israel, there to visit and reconnect with family. So the last thing I expected to see when

I stopped for a cup of coffee was carnage."

"Carnage? You mean like dead bodies?"

"Like dead bodies."

"Were there lots?"

"I had no idea at first, because it was hard to tell who was dead and who was injured. But there was a lot of screaming and a lot of debris—and a lot of people on the ground, bleeding."

5 DAVID

The dirt and the stench of blood and excrement had been overshadowed by screams and cries for help. "After a shard of something—probably glass from a broken window—nicked my forehead, I rushed from the coffee shop, intent only on seeing what I could do to help. The other patrons ran every which way, a few into the chaos beside me."

He closed his eyes momentarily. "Your mother was the first person I came across after the explosion. I had no way of knowing then that nineteen people died that day. Four of those were children waiting with their mother for the bus."

Tony looked at Meira. "Kids?" His voice went up an octave. "Dead?"

"And dozens injured."

1979

Some of the settling dust had fallen on David. He'd never witnessed destruction like this, not even in the Navy, where he'd trained other pilots instead of going to war. He'd been good at it, so he'd lucked out, then—and now.

But these poor people hadn't.

He bent over a young woman and offered help. She protested before allowing him to carry her to his car. She was a stunning creature, in spite of the blood and dirt on her face. In spite of her almost mannish clothing. None of that took away from those huge eyes with those incredibly long lashes. Lashes that were real.

Like her curves. And the texture of her skin under the dust. With lips that—

Meira's interruption pulled him back. "David, my turn to remind you of your audience."

"Yeah, Dad."

Was that a trace of real humor in Tony's smirk? David grinned back, just in case. "Sorry. I got a little carried away," he said. "I'll keep it kid-friendly, but I think my attraction to your mother was how HaShem pointed her out as my future wife."

David chose to ignore Tony's curled lip and concentrate on making this a love story their son would remember. His own parents' romance had kept him focused on the end game and made him unwilling to settle for less than they'd had. Maybe it would work the same way for Tony—eventually.

"Back to Jerusalem and the aftermath of the bombing."

FROM FIRE INTO FIRE

1979

David tried to carry the woman loosely so as not to jar her injured leg, but he needed to get her to safety in case another bomb went off. Grateful he'd parked far enough away that he'd be able to get to the car without running afoul of police and rescue vehicles, he headed down the block and around a corner.

"We're almost to my rental."

She nodded against his chest. "*Toda*. Thank you."

"By the way, I'm David Rassadim."

"Meira. Meira Barash."

"I'd rather the circumstances were different, but I'm glad to meet you."

She blushed. He could see the red even through the dust coating her face. If anything, that blush sealed it for him.

And there sat the car, untouched by the havoc behind them. But how to get her in and settled? He shot up a prayer. *Suggestions?*

He'd no more than thought the request when a man approached and asked, "May I help?"

David smiled, both at the man and toward the sky. "My right front pocket. The keys." He lifted the woman away from his side to give the man access.

"Back seat?" the man who might have been an angel asked.

"I think so."

"Blood," she said. "Your car."

"Ah, yes. There's a jacket on the passenger seat."

Soon, the door was open, and the man spread out the jacket and helped slide Meira into the seat. Her big eyes registered pain, but she bit her bottom lip.

To stifle a moan? To appear brave? David squeezed her

hand and sighed to himself when she squeezed back.

"Thank you," she said, her voice wavering. "Thank you both."

The other man waved and hurried off, perhaps to help others. David climbed in behind the wheel. "Will you give me directions? I am merely a tourist here."

"American?"

He grinned at that. Of course, she'd heard the non-native in his speech. "New York."

"The city?"

"Only occasionally. Mostly upstate."

She told him where to turn, how to get to her father's home. And when they arrived, she waited in the car while he rang her father's doorbell.

He brushed excess dust from his shirt and slacks and used his sleeve to clean as much from his face as he could while he waited, hating that he'd have to turn her over to her family. To say goodbye.

An aproned woman opened the door. *"Shalom,"* he said, "I have Meira Barash in the car. She's been injured."

The woman's hand flew to her mouth, and she peered around him. "Oh, the poor darling. Come, come. Bring her. I will find her father, her mother. You bring her into the house." She dashed away, leaving the door open.

He returned to the car. Meira helped again, scooting back toward him using her good leg until he was able to hoist her out with one arm around her waist, the other ready to cradle her legs again. He was grateful she was neither heavy nor tall, but instead fit perfectly against him. "That's good. Just hang on," he said as she circled his neck with her arm. She turned when he eased her out so she could hold onto him and he could again stand with her. Her satchel slammed against his side, but she didn't seem to notice. By the time they reached the house, two women met them.

An older gentleman appeared behind the women, waved him forward, and said in Hebrew, "This way. Give the man room."

"She's bleeding," David said, eyeing the sofa. "A towel under her leg?"

The one who must have been Meira's mother grabbed what looked like a knitted blanket and spread it on the upholstered surface. As David lowered his burden and set down her bag, Mrs. Barash spoke to the aproned woman. "Bina, would you please bring warm water, a cloth, and towels?"

David extended his hand to the father. "David Rassadim. I came across your daughter just after the blast. She didn't want me to take her to the hospital."

"The hospitals are probably overflowing. We will allow her mother to see to the wounds and decide if Meira needs a doctor. You will come with me, please?" He bent over his daughter and bussed her forehead. "I will want to hear all after your mother examines you. Yes?"

"Ken, yes." Meira looked over at David. "Thank you so much for all you've done."

"I'm glad I could help." He smiled, wishing he could say more, do more. Then he followed her father out and across the hall.

"Perhaps you would like to wash first? You, too, have a wound."

"Thank you, I would. Mr. Barash." David spoke the name almost as an afterthought. To show respect and to imprint it.

He didn't want to forget her name. Ever.

"Eban, please." Meira's father indicated another door at the end of the hall. "I will await you here in my library."

David cleaned up as best he could without soiling one of the luxurious towels set aside for guests. The cut in his forehead had stopped bleeding, but he could do with a shower and a change of clothes.

The library smelled of old books and leather overlaid with something that must have been furniture polish. David stood, awkwardly aware of the dirt still clinging to his slacks.

Eban pointed him to one of the large leather chairs. "Please, be seated."

As the older man moved to a sideboard, David studied his appearance: the tailored slacks, the pressed white shirt, the thick head of still-dark hair. Meira's father looked like a man who wielded power.

Eban switched to British-accented English. "May I offer you a drink? Scotch? It is something I learned to enjoy during my time in England." At David's "Yes, please," he lifted the decanter top, poured two fingers' worth in each glass, and handed one to David.

Back home, David would have asked for ice. Or a beer. He took a small sip and tried not to wince when the fire hit his throat. "Thank you."

"I am grateful to you for helping my daughter." Eban eased into the other large chair and lifted his glass in salute.

"I happened to be at the right place at the right moment. Anyone would have done the same."

"I disagree and consider it an unusual kindness that, instead of running away, you brought her home." The older man contemplated the amber liquor in his glass before sipping.

FROM FIRE INTO FIRE

"You are an American. I find that interesting. I have never visited America, although I attended school in Britain and have encouraged my two children to learn other languages. English and Arabic. Also French. These are good for them, here and abroad."

"Do you and your family travel often?" Maybe if he made conversation, it would open a door for him to visit again. To become acquainted with this man's daughter. With Meira.

What a beautiful name. *Light*. Had her parents considered its meaning when they named her? Because it fit. He couldn't imagine her being called anything else.

Her smile certainly lit something in him.

And wasn't that a puzzle? Oh, he'd been lit up by women before, but only on the surface, like a damp match that sparked and then fizzled. This felt different. It reminded him of the flame in one of those little cans of cooking fuel that could boil soup and keep it simmering for hours when the electricity went off.

Eban seemed ready to talk, but he did so slowly, sometimes sipping, sometimes contemplating his glass. "We enjoy travel and do so when we can, especially to England where my son is doing post-graduate work. We have been through much of Europe, including my wife's hometown just outside of Munich. Of her family, only she and her mother survived the war, and her mother died soon after."

"The camps?" The thought of them made his gut twist. It always did.

"Dachau. They called it a labor camp. It wasn't."

"I'm so sorry. I can't imagine."

"No. Nor I. But you, you don't have a Jewish surname."

"Armenian. My grandfather. He married a girl from Jaffa

who raised their children in the Jewish tradition. They eventually went to the United States, but my father came here at the end of WWII to study at the Hebrew University. He married an Israeli and took her back to New York with him. I was born in the States."

"So you have dual citizenship?"

"I do."

"And I imagine you have relatives still here."

David laughed. "More than I can count, on both sides."

"That too is a good thing. My poor wife has none, but I have many, so my children have a family. That is important."

Tony stopped him with a lifted hand. "Whoa. Dual citizenship? You're Israeli?"

"And American."

"I thought you were just American. Like me."

"Well—"

"Not yet." Meira raised a brow, reminding him to back away from that conversation.

David nodded. "I was about to tell your grandfather about my uncle, Avram Katz, with whom I was staying. You haven't met him yet, but I'm sure you will someday."

"He's Israeli." Tony looked as glum as he sounded.

"Yes. Your grandfather knew who my Uncle Avram was, and the relationship seemed to please him, so he asked me more about myself, where I'd gone to school."

"Did you tell him true stuff?"

"I did. I told him about my graduate degree from Cornell, my stint in the Navy, my engineering job. He invited me to dinner the next day."

"I thought you went to that place with the initials."

"You mean MIT? I did, for my doctorate, but I hadn't received more than a master's when I met your mother. My doctorate came later."

"I guess Nono liked you 'cause you're smart."

"My romance with your mother seems to have been pushed by both your grandfather and my uncle."

Meira laughed. "Mutual admiration society."

"It seemed that way." He grinned at her before turning back to Tony. "The night after I met your mother, I discovered Uncle Avram's prejudice in her favor. I told my uncle about her, and when I mentioned your grandfather's name, he grew quiet, puffing and slowly blowing out the smoke. Then he said, 'Eban Barash?' like I'd hit the jackpot."

"'Cause he was in government?" Tony asked.

David nodded. "A powerful man, it seemed. My uncle's pleasure got me wondering if my meeting your mother was anything like Isaac's servant encountering Rebecca at the well."

"Who's Isaac?"

Meira raised her brows. "Our son needs some religious training."

"No, I don't," Tony said, waving the idea away like a fly in front of his face.

"Every educated person should know the Bible stories," David said, "whether you choose to believe them or not."

Tony blew out a puff of air.

David ignored him. "Isaac was one of the patriarchs. The son of Abraham, to whom Adonai promised generations of sons to carry the message of the Holy One. We'll tell you more about him later."

"I know about Abraham. Ishmael was his first son. The Arabs came from him, and Allah loved him best."

The influences that had been pummeling Tony with lies angered David, and yet he and Meira had given them access by positioning their son so he'd be vulnerable. And now they had to fix it—or at least try. "Who told you that?"

"Bahir's tutor. Sometimes he went with us to the beach and told us stories."

"Well, here's the truth—"

Tony shot to his feet, his face reddening and his hands becoming fists at his sides. *"Truth?* Whose truth? Bahir never, *ever* lied to me."

"Sit down, son." David spoke quietly but with a coolness that demanded obedience.

Tony stared at the floor, his fingers stuck in his front pockets, his shoulders hunched. Finally, he fell back onto the couch.

Meira reached over to grab David's hand. Her eyes reflected the sorrow he felt as she directed her words at their son. "Truth is an absolute. Just because we haven't told it to you earlier—and you'll better understand why as we continue the story—doesn't change truth, certainly not the truth of Scripture. Abraham's firstborn was indeed Ishmael, but Ishmael was the son of a concubine—a servant—not of his wife. Ishmael was born because Abraham and his wife Sarah stopped trusting in HaShem and His promises. He was born because of their unbelief."

Tony didn't look up, and he didn't speak.

"That's a conversation for another day," David said. "Back to our tale. My Uncle Avram worked for the Ministry of Public Security and, as I said, knew your grandfather. Connections are crucial, no matter where you live, but especially in a small country like Israel. I figured my uncle would foster my relationship with your mother because of her father. Her father might do the same because of my uncle."

"Tell him about your mother," Meira said. "You know, the story she told me after we were married."

David grinned. "He's going to make us promise never to play matchmaker."

That provoked a raised eyebrow when Tony looked at him. At least they'd gotten his attention. "Matchmaker?"

"My parents," David continued, "especially my mom, wanted me to follow in my father's footsteps and bring home a bride from Israel, but this was 1979, not the 1940s when my dad went to Jerusalem to study—and to marry. My mother wouldn't let it alone. She was so determined I find a nice Israeli bride that she wrote to at least half the extended family. I ended up meeting girl friends of cousins, girls who were second, third, and fourth cousins, anyone who seemed remotely marriageable."

"Yuck."

"Yeah, well, that's about how I felt," David said. "Until I met your mother. At first, I thought she was only a chance-met woman, but it didn't take me long to decide chance had nothing to do with it."

Tony looked from one of them to the other. "Are you talking about luck or fortune-telling kind of stuff?"

"God kind of stuff."

"So what'd you do?"

"I only had another week of vacation, and I lived 5900 miles away. Of course, I had no idea a madman would force my hand."

"Force it?" Meira narrowed her eyes in a scowl.

Laughing, David drew her to him. The embrace wasn't

smoothly done, but he made his point and surprised a laugh from her. Normally, Tony would have grinned with them. He didn't.

"Let's say," David said when she'd straightened again, "what happened next brought us to the point sooner rather than later."

6 MEIRA

Tony let out an exasperated sigh. "Can we, you know, get off all the mush?"

"Fine, no more mush," David said, draping his arm around Meira's shoulders. "Back to the bad-guy stuff."

She turned to press her back against her husband, needing his closeness. "My turn," she said. "The day after the bombing, I went in to teach my classes as usual."

"What about your leg?" Tony asked.

"The doctor stitched me up, and my mother insisted I use my grandfather's cane if I wouldn't stay home and in bed. I'd have loved to take the day off, but my students had a project due, so my father dropped me off at the school and said he'd come back for me at the end of the day." Remembering her foolishness, her lack of forethought, she sighed. "I could have avoided all that came next if I'd used my brain. Instead, I made it simple for the bomber to identify me."

"How come?" Tony asked, suddenly more interested.

"Are you asking why I did it or how?"

"Both."

"The why remains a mystery, even to me. The how? I didn't connect the dots. I knew he'd seen my face, and he'd seen it within half a block of the school. All he had to do was hang around the area to see if he could spot me coming or going from a house or a business on that street. I should have assumed he'd try to find out who I was so he could silence me."

Tony glanced from her to his father and back. "How come your dad didn't make you stay home?"

Recounting this part still embarrassed her. "Because I hadn't told him or anyone that I'd seen the man's face."

"That was dumb," her son said with all the wisdom of his thirteen years.

"It was incredibly dumb." And all the rest had come from that one stupid choice, hadn't it? "When I went out to pick up lunch from the sandwich shop across the street, the bomber was leaning against a no-parking sign. He blended so well with my students in his jeans and t-shirt that I didn't recognize him until I headed back toward the school and he turned in my direction. I almost tripped over my cane, I was so surprised."

"Oh, man, you must have been scared to death."

She had been. Her heart had raced, and sweat had pooled under her arms once she was on the other side of the school door. "I got into the building before he could do anything. When I looked out the window of the school office, I saw he had cornered a couple of my students."

Tony beat a tattoo on his knees with his fingertips. "What did they tell him?"

She wanted to grab his hands to stop their fidgets, but instead she focused on his face. "He pretended to know me from university and got one of them to say my name."

"Just like that? Sounds really stupid. I mean, if he wasn't a Jew like them."

"Not all my students were Jewish. Some were Arabs, although most spoke Hebrew as well as Arabic and even English. They had no suspicion he was the bomber, so it would have been easy to involve them in conversation."

"Like I said, dumb."

"On my part," she said, "not theirs. I called the police, gave them a sketch of the man's face, and had my father pick me up in a taxi."

"Was Nono mad?"

"At me? He was furious."

༄

1979

Her father waited to speak until he'd helped her into the house, set her carryall on the floor, and led her into his library. "Now. What is this all about?"

She leaned the walking stick against the wall and eased down onto one of his big chairs, cudgeling her brain for words that wouldn't worry him. There weren't any, not with a man who could extract truth with that unflinching stare of his faster than a dentist could yank out a tooth—and sometimes with equal pain. Aba had been winning contests of wills against her and Yaacov since they'd first tried to deny misbehavior. He always won. Always.

"The man who set the bomb knows my name."

Aba began to pace. When she got to the end of her narrative, he looked down at her over his long nose, his bushy brows jutting over narrowed eyes. "Why didn't you tell me he'd seen you? And near your school? I would have told you not to present yourself in that neighborhood for fear just such a thing would happen."

The control in his voice sent a shiver through her. She'd have preferred a more visible anger, because suddenly the ramifications of her choices seemed more deadly than she'd imagined. She hadn't thought, had she, and now she'd put them all in danger.

"I'm sorry, Aba."

"I know you are." He sighed, walked to the sideboard, and poured himself a finger of scotch. "Now we must decide what to do," he said, taking a sip. "Let me think about it and discuss this with your mother. I will also speak with the police."

Meira stood and headed for the door. He stopped her, saying, "I have invited that young man, David Rassadim, to dine with us tonight."

She shouldn't have been surprised, although she couldn't help the jolt that hit her at his words. Her parents would naturally offer hospitality to someone who had helped a member of the family. She nodded and headed upstairs.

Her father's disappointment kicked her worry into high gear. In trying to hang onto a semblance of freedom, she'd endangered everyone.

She turned on the bathroom faucet and waited for the water to warm. Her reflection stared back from the mirror above the sink, her normally smooth forehead riddled with worry lines. She imagined them deepening, turning her hag-like before she was thirty.

FROM FIRE INTO FIRE

Just when she wanted to be beautiful.

Because *he* was coming. She splashed her face, wiped it dry, and hurried into her bedroom.

After rejecting one dress and then the next and the next, her fingers rested on the deep purple crepe that draped in layers to just below the knee. Ima didn't approve of the American short skirts, but she wanted her daughter to be stylish. Most days, Meira ignored her mother's wince at her choice of pants—a dress would not work in the studio—but tonight she needed to feel beautiful, and that meant a swirly dress, even if her poor battered leg wouldn't be happy balancing in heels.

She pulled off her khakis and top and slid the silky dress over her head, smoothing it down over her hips and reaching behind to zip it up the back. Wiggling, she could almost reach the top of the zipper, but Ima would have to help with those last few inches to make her presentable for their guest.

She shouldn't be thinking this way, not about a man when there was all that other hanging over her head, over her family's head. But she didn't want to wallow in guilt tonight. Or worry about anyone's safety.

She wanted to see David again. Their guest. Who happened to be an American. She wanted to feel pretty and admired even if only for one evening.

The distance between here and America was a good thing. It meant he'd soon be gone, and she could forget about him.

That was what she wanted, wasn't it? Just this evening. No involvement, and after that, her life as it had been.

But it would never be that again. Not after the mess she'd made by forgetting she had brains—or by forgetting to use them.

She sat in front of her dressing-table mirror and brushed her hair until the table light gleamed in its auburn strands. The action of drawing the brush down and through was automatic, drilled into her by her mother—one hundred strokes (but who counted) to bring out the shine. As a child, she'd watched her mother's nightly ritual and thought how beautiful her mother's curls were when they bounced as the brush loosed them. Her sweet Ima, whose life Meira might have endangered by her recklessness today.

She checked the time. An hour yet to wait with nothing to do. Bina wouldn't want her in the kitchen. Ima was probably closeted with Aba, talking about her and the afternoon's disaster.

She moved to her small bookcase and took out one of her reference books. She'd be teaching a class on the Impressionists next term. Perhaps she should use this time to study up on the period.

She flipped through a few pages, unable to focus on art, but she did her best, flipping and staring for a good quarter hour. Her watch showed she still had thirty-three minutes to go.

Fine. Maybe she'd go down early, get her mother to pull up her zipper all the way. She mustn't forget the zipper.

Wouldn't that be embarrassing, the top of her dress folded down on itself, her back gaping for all to see? She grabbed her tube of lip gloss and dabbed some on, checking the color. It worked. Her cheeks had pink that flamed too easily—and they'd add even more if she grew tongue-tied talking to the man.

David.

Tony's groan yanked her from the memory. Poor thing had his head in his hands.

"Take a deep breath, son. She's not giving you any details, so you can relax," David said. "But we'll move on. Your mom stayed home over the next few days while plans to keep everyone safe were in the works. Finally, using Mom's sketches, the police arrested a suspect. We thought that was the end of it. She'd identify the guy. He'd go to prison. Thinking it was over, we grew complacent."

They hadn't, she thought. *She* had. "Much too complacent."

Tony's knee started to bounce.

"Just a little more, and we'll take a break."

He stopped the bouncing. "I don't need a break. Just tell me what happened."

"Fine," she said, because agreeing was easier. She'd call a halt soon, whether he wanted one or not. "I relaxed when I shouldn't have and didn't think beyond the moment, assuming an arrest meant we were all safe."

"Why didn't it?" The bouncing started again, this time with the other leg.

She ignored it. "They had the wrong man. My father's plan was to pick me up at the school so I could identify the suspect once the police said they were ready for me. My morning class went as usual, and I decided to enjoy the warm weather and loosen some of the kinks in my muscles by taking a short walk. The secretary would tell my father where I was if he called."

"By the time I got there to check on you, your father had already left to get you," David said. "I couldn't believe you'd actually gone back to the school."

"I saw no reason not to. No bomber, no danger." She shrugged. "Going outside, though, was reckless. I admit it. For one thing, I'd been injured. For another, I had no idea if the bomber had worked alone. Common sense and I had parted company, and I didn't think beyond how bright the sun was that day and how much I needed to move, injury or not. You know how much I love to walk. I couldn't resist pulling on my sweater and hobbling around the block."

"At least you had the sweater and the cane." David's gentle squeeze felt comforting.

"If it hadn't been for those and for my father driving up at that exact moment..."

"What?" Tony asked. "What would have happened?"

"Your mother would have been killed."

"Kill-ed?" His boy's voice cracked into a soprano, and his legs stilled. "Re-ally?"

She nodded. "I had just turned toward your grandfather's car when a man came at me with a knife. I guess the cane in my hand and the fact that I was in the middle of my turn gave me an advantage and deflected that nasty blade, so I ended up with a slashed arm and an unraveled sweater instead of a pierced stomach and, if the knife had continued upward, a hole in my heart." The memory of the attacker's words also stuck. "He cried '*Allahu Akbar*' as he slashed at me, and I recognized him. It was the bomber."

"Whoa. Is that where you got that scar on your arm? You said it was 'cause of an accident."

"Now you know." She smoothed back his hair. "You could say it was an accident that the knife only sliced my arm, because he'd certainly intended worse."

Tony ducked away from her hand. "Yeah, right. So, did they get him? The guy with the knife?"

"No. There was too much confusion at the scene. I lost my

balance and fell to the sidewalk, bleeding and awkward. People rushed forward to help. I don't think anyone knew immediately what had happened, or who'd done it, so the attacker got away."

"Then who was the guy in jail?"

"A look-alike cousin," she said. "Another would-be freedom fighter."

David snorted. "You mean terrorist. Let's not honor them with a name they don't deserve. They weren't fighting for freedom. They lived in freedom."

"Which allowed them access to me and the others," Meira said.

Tony frowned and said, "But those guys were Palestinians?"

"They were Arab Israelis."

"Who'd lost their homeland." Back was his mulish look.

"No," she said, "they hadn't. The bomber and his cousin lived in family homes in and around Nazareth. They were Israeli citizens."

"Second-class citizens," he said, with all the fierceness of a budding rebel.

Meira sighed. "I imagine they'd been taught to believe that, but most of my Arab students appreciated the standard of living and education available to them, which was, and still is, much higher than in the surrounding Arab countries."

David intervened. "We can debate the politics of the area later. Right now, we have a story to tell, and whatever personal grievances those young men believed they had, they were determined to silence your mother by killing her."

She couldn't let it go, not yet. "Too many of them have been raised to believe all Jews should be forced into the sea just because we're Jews."

"Because the Jews took their homeland." Tony's tone made her want to cuff him. She'd never hit him, but had he ever been this belligerent toward them?

She took a deep breath and released it slowly. She needed calm. They'd tried to help Tony learn to be open-minded and accepting, but he'd been surrounded for years by those who looked at Israel with jaundiced eyes, too often red-veined with hatred.

David firmed his grip on her. "This isn't the time for that debate."

"You're right. I'm sorry." She longed for some of his patience, wishing it would transfer through touch. "So, then. After the doctor stitched up my arm and I stopped in at the police station to assure them that the man behind bars wasn't the bomber, we realized we'd better implement some plan that would actually keep us all safe."

"You get that, don't you?" David asked Tony. "A murderer running loose who knew your mother's family name put them all in danger, not just Mom. Especially because your grandfather was a member of the Knesset, the Israeli parliament. His job was important enough to make him a prime target."

"Nono?" Tony's eyes widened, but then he returned to the sneer that made him singularly unattractive and not at all like her son. Meira wanted to take a washcloth and scrub it off. "I guess that's not so important in a tiny country like Israel, not like in America."

"Your grandfather," David said, his voice growing softer as it always did when he was trying to control his anger, "held an important position in the *only* democracy in the Middle East.

Keep that in mind when you spout the party line of your former classmates."

Tony hung his head, but he didn't respond. Into that silence, the phone rang.

Meira sighed. "Mr. Holloway, Dean of Students at the Belvedere School, phoned while you were outside. He wants to know when we can bring Tony to see the school."

Tony pulled a throw pillow to his chest. "Never. Tell him 'never.' I don't want to go to some dumb boarding school."

David put up a hand to stop Tony's words. "We'll call him later. Let's take a break for a little while. I'll get us something to drink."

Good. They needed to put this discussion on pause. Before she said something she'd regret.

David slid his strong arms around her as she leaned back against the counter. "Come here, you."

She clung to him. "It's so hard."

"I know, love." He nuzzled her hair, bringing his lips to her forehead and then moving them slowly down her cheek. "You smell of verbena," he whispered before lifting her chin so his lips could touch hers, lightly, sweetly, and then deeply.

He straightened, still holding her close. "I want to tell our son how it felt for me, falling in love with you, fearing for you. I want him to know it all from my perspective, a foreigner in Israel who saw first-hand what it was like."

She nodded into his shoulder. "Then you should tell him, but it probably won't mean much to him now. Not yet, anyway."

"But maybe he'll think about it in years to come. How HaShem brought us together. How the Lord protected us."

Meira pulled away and looked up at him. "Have we done a disservice to our faith? After this, will Tony ever accept who he is? Who we are?"

"He's still young. We have years to help him past the shock of this discovery."

"But we won't be here."

"We'll be here for the rest of the summer, for every vacation, and any time he needs us."

She wanted to believe him—and David obviously wanted to convince himself. They should have told Tony sooner, when young meant malleable, tractable. But then they would have had to send him away to school sooner.

And she hadn't been able to stand that thought, had she? So they'd waited. She prayed they hadn't waited too long.

"Two more months before we give him over to a school," she said. "That's not a lot of time."

David closed his eyes. She imagined him agreeing. Regretting. Thinking two months wasn't much time at all.

She glanced toward the living room. "He needs to go do something active. Is it too hot for you guys to jog?"

"Much." David didn't look like he wanted even to consider movement.

"His legs are jittery. He needs exercise."

"Fine. I'll take him out to shoot a few hoops." He grabbed two of the glasses and led the way into the living room.

Tony sat with his feet propped against the rough-hewn coffee table and his head almost ninety degrees from his chest. The kid looked like a candidate for scoliosis.

"Sit up," David said, extending a glass of water.

Tony grunted, but he sat up and reached for it.

"Bring your water. I'm challenging you to a game of one-on-one."

And, suddenly, Tony was an eager kid again, his animosity forgotten in the promise of basketball. Until David said, "One thing you can't do in Beirut, right?"

The glower flashed back in an instant. "I can do anything there. Lots of people play basketball."

David returned the look and the tone. "At your school? With Bahir?"

"We do sometimes. We can play anytime we want." Tony'd flipped back to anger. "They have a league for big kids. Teams. Here's not so special."

Meira stepped between them. "Go on, both of you. Work off your frustration outside, please. With the ball."

7 Meira

She stood at the open window as the two males in her life pummeled the backboard and the asphalt. David was obviously trying to make up for his tongue-slip, but Tony didn't look as if his mood had softened, not if those ball slams were any indication.

She felt the same sick guilt and regret she'd known as a girl when she'd skipped school and her father'd called her to his library. The disappointment on Aba's face had been harder to bear than any whipping he might have meted out.

Would her son continue to wear that same betrayed expression? Would he hate his parents with equal fervor to the love he'd felt?

She and David had told themselves the years of playacting in Lebanon had borne fruit and saved lives. Just last month,

David had overheard a conversation between a couple of radical professors who'd thought him too engrossed in filling his plate from the buffet to notice them half-hidden behind palm fronds. They'd mentioned a name and a location, a name David knew. He'd passed this information to his Israeli contacts, who'd uncovered bomb-making supplies at the address, along with blueprints of a Haifa resort and plans for an attack at the height of the tourist season.

She'd contributed, too, through the art classes she taught and from the university wives she met. Only, the toll those years had taken and would continue to take would not be worth it if it cost them Tony. With each passing year, her worry had grown. It was one thing to lie to an enemy. It was a completely different matter to lie to one's son. One's friends.

Had it only been a week ago Saturday that the apartment door had slammed open, and Tony had stumbled in, bleeding from his nose and a cut on his lip, one eye swollen, with ravages of tears streaking his cheeks? "Bahir. Help Bahir. Downstairs."

The boys had been playing on the beach near the apartment when the bullies attacked. From Tony's description, David determined the teens had been members of Hezbollah from the poverty stricken Shiite minority.

David had gotten Bahir home while she'd patched up Tony. And then they'd begun the process that had brought them here.

They'd completed his enrollment application to the school they'd found, one that was far, far from madmen. It had been past time to take this step, because in spite of attending the American School in Beirut, Tony'd begun to spout liberationist propaganda. "Jews stole the land belonging to the

FROM FIRE INTO FIRE

Palestinians," he'd said one afternoon when she'd been his only audience. "They have no right to be there."

It had been all she could do not to weep in front of him. She'd imagined the horror of watching Tony grow to espouse a philosophy meant to destroy his own people. It couldn't be allowed to happen. And yet, they'd dawdled, thinking they had time. Until the beach incident had upped the ante.

Enrolling him in a boarding school had always been part of the plan, but not this way. There'd always seemed to be time. Until there wasn't. But surely, it wouldn't take him long to find American friends and learn to be an American boy. Instead of a pretend Arab.

They'd left behind a promising connection David had made through Bahir's pacifist father, Nasri Ramah, an economics professor at the American University of Beirut where David taught engineering. Nasri had introduced David to a leftist professor sympathetic—and perhaps more than sympathetic—to Iranian-backed Hezbollah, a group determined to see the destruction of Israel. The man might have led David to other plots and other knowledge.

Whether or not she and David returned to Lebanon would depend on how this time at the lake cottage resolved itself. Tony had to be their number one priority. He should always have been.

The evening before their flight home, she'd fled to their balcony to breathe the sea air while Tony said goodbye to a bruised and battered Bahir. Through the open door, she'd heard the boys promise eternal friendship, and her heart had ached for them.

How she longed for a world where boys weren't threatened and her family in Israel could imagine peace from its neighbors. Where she could be certain that bad guys weren't still trying to kill her and hers.

Her son's voice brought her back to the present and the interaction happening just outside the kitchen window. "Come on, Dad, shoot!" Tony called.

David tossed the ball, and in it went. He retrieved it easily and made another basket, but then he slowed down, and Tony grabbed the ball from him, dribbled, and made a wild throw.

"Almost got it," David said in the rah-rah tone of a cheerleader.

"Yeah, right."

David extended the ball. "Here, try again."

"It's not my turn." But Tony took it.

"Let's just practice. Work on your aim."

Tony listened as his father gave him pointers on his stance and his aim in the free throw. After three misses, David said, "Relax. I think you're trying too hard."

Biting his bottom lip, Tony closed his eyes for a moment, then looked at the board and tossed the ball. He was way off.

Meira had seen him make multiple baskets in a row, but today he could barely seem to hit the backboard, while his father couldn't seem to miss. Their normally easy-going son looked ready to explode.

Perhaps she should intervene, break up the tension with a distraction. But, no, David had played basketball with his son since Tony could first hold the ball. They needed to work this out between themselves.

Turning from the window, she opened the refrigerator, got out hummus, dill pickles, and spinach, then went into the pantry cupboard for the pita bread. She'd spread one sandwich when a screech came from Tony.

FROM FIRE INTO FIRE

David's frustrated "What the—what are you doing?" came in response.

She ran to the back door, pushed it open, and arrived in the yard in time to see Tony dash around to the lakeside with a "Leave me alone" shouted over his shoulder. David plowed his fingers through his hair.

"What?" she asked.

David crouched on his haunches. "I keep blowing it."

"Tell me."

"I tried to encourage him, talked about the school. The things he can do next year."

"And?"

"I don't know. Something ticked him off." David stood and waved toward the side of the house. "He kicked the ball as hard as he could. I'd better go check on him."

She followed, expecting to see Tony on the porch or maybe down at the dock. "Could he have gone inside?" she asked.

"You check. I'll head to the dock. See if I can spot him anywhere."

Meira opened the door and stood at the entrance, listening. At first, there was only silence, and then the toilet flushed. She returned to the porch and hailed David. "He's in here."

Waving, David continued to the sandy bank of the lake and bent down to retrieve something. When he stood, he carried the basketball under his arm. His frown had intensified.

She waited by the screen door for him to join her, and they went inside together. David set the ball down on the closet floor.

"His behavior is unacceptable," he said.

"I know. But he probably thinks ours is too."

"He has no right to judge us."

"David."

He raked his fingers through his hair and, on a sigh, moved toward her. Drawing her into his arms, he pressed her close. "This hurts." His voice was ragged. "It just hurts."

Her cheek rested against his damp shirt, next to his beating heart, and the thurump-thurump of it adjusted hers to match its rhythm. She could feel it, feel their unity of purpose, of being. "I know," she whispered as she smoothed her palm up to his neck and to his cheek. "It will be okay. It will."

The bathroom door opened, and, sucking in a deep breath, David shifted back. Tony paused uncertainly when he saw them.

"Let's eat," Meira said. "It's almost ready." Anything to diffuse the tension.

Another sigh came from her husband. And then he seemed to get a whiff of himself. "Perhaps a quick wash-up first, before I overwhelm you with my manly odor."

"You're fine," she said.

"Sorry, but we're both rank." He motioned Tony toward the bathroom. "You first . . . and don't use all the hot water."

Tony's glance stunned her with its shy hopefulness. He must know he'd overstepped his bounds and probably couldn't believe he'd been given a pass. Yes, he owed his father an apology, but David would have to be the one to demand it.

Unless David hoped that it would be offered freely.

Tony wasn't a child any longer, even if he still looked younger than his thirteen years. Thirteen, growing, and now confronted with a life change that might make his teenage angst flip into overdrive. And they, instead of helping him navigate these years, seemed to be making a mess of things. With head bowed, she begged the Lord for mercy. For help. For peace in her family and peace in their boy's soul.

Five minutes after the pipes had stopped creaking and groaning, she filled the glasses with ice and drinks. Soda was on treat status for Tony because of its caffeinated sugar, but maybe it would counteract all the unpalatable truths they'd been doling out, sweet for sour. She and David preferred tea.

David slid an arm around her and planted a kiss on her cheek before grabbing a bag of chips and a stack of napkins.

"You holding up?"

"Trying to. You?"

"Tiptoeing through this." He nodded toward the tray of drinks and sandwiches. "I'll get that."

He led the way into the living room and set the tray down on the coffee table. Meira followed with plates and chips, taking a comfortable chair opposite the couch.

Tony stood as if waiting for permission to join them. David didn't give it. Instead, he watched his son.

"I'm sorry," Tony finally said, his head bowed. "I shouldn't have gotten so mad."

"Temper tantrums are never acceptable," David said, not giving an inch. Then he softened his words., "Anger in itself is not wrong. Just what you do with it."

"Yes, sir."

"Come. Sit down and have some lunch." David slid Tony's drink down the table. "Perhaps we ought to talk about what went wrong out there."

"Do we have to?" Tony asked.

"Seems to me you were too upset to play well. And then you got mad at yourself, more than at me."

"I guess."

"Fine, we'll leave it alone for now. You've apologized, and I assume that means you'll try to control your temper."

Tony nodded.

Delighted with both her men, Meira had been putting sandwiches on plates. She extended one to Tony. "You were shooting baskets on your own while I fixed dinner last night, and you got most of them in. Where'd you learn to shoot like that?"

Tony grinned. "Sometimes Hussam, Bahir's tutor, takes us to the gym where he plays. He's on a team."

She passed the napkins. "This tutor, is he for religion?"

"Math. Bahir's dad wants him to go to Harvard 'cause that's where he went."

"Interesting," Meira said. "I wonder why his mother never mentioned it."

"She wants to keep him home." Tony reached for a handful of chips and piled them on his plate.

"Mothers are protective," David said. "Dads, too, but perhaps not in the same way. Besides, Harvard is a good school."

"Maybe we could both go." Tony's expression held longing.

"If it works out that way." *Please no.* But she didn't say that.

"I suppose it depends on which school meets your needs at the time. Now, before we eat, we must thank God for the food we have received. Tony?" David waited. "This will be new for you, but you need to become accustomed to hearing Hebrew prayers instead of Muslim ones."

Tony's head jerked up. His face closed down.

"Listen to the words. They are not only beautiful, but also

full of meaning." David waited to begin his prayer until the boy bit his lip and lowered his eyes.

"*Barukh ata Adonai Eloheinu melekh ha'olam hamotzi lehem min ha'aretz.* Blessed are You, Lord our God, King of the Universe, Who brings forth bread from the earth." David repeated the blessing over the other parts of the meal.

"Amen," Meira said. "And so we give thanks."

"I don't." Tony's voice vibrated with a scorn that banished the few moments of peace they'd shared.

Meira ducked her head again and tried to grab hold of what she'd experienced during David's prayer. *Blessed are You, Adonai. Help our boy. Have mercy. Have mercy.*

She picked up her sandwich, bit into it, and chewed. Chewing worked. Swallowing was harder.

Just get it finished. Get through it. "Joy comes in the morning." Of course, it was only noon. She wasn't sure she could wait until morning, not even a metaphorical one.

8 Meira

Meira focused on the need to finish what they'd begun instead of on her son's attitude. Or at least, she tried to, because what she wanted to do was forget everything and walk around the lake—or even grab a book and put up the hammock. At the end of the hall, her studio waited for her, the perfect place to create and lose herself.

Soon. Once they'd finished this. Once Tony had forgiven her.

She'd imagined herself a good mother, a kind one, educated, talented. Now she felt like a mom-failure, a woman looking to excuse choices she'd made.

But, if she'd learned one thing, it was that quitting never worked.

"I will tell you more of our story, if you'd like. Even if you wouldn't, I'll still tell you." She looked for at least a sliver of a grin, but Tony focused on his plate. With a sigh, she said, "Your grandfather decided we needed to leave Jerusalem while the bomber was still at large, and so he took us to a hotel on the beach at Tel Aviv, quite a luxurious one."

"A hotel on the beach is kind of neat."

David pointed to her sandwich, as if to suggest she eat. "We were all trying to come up with a solution that would offer the needed protection," he said. "I knew what I wanted, and I'd spoken with my uncle and my mother's cousin, a high-ranking rabbi, but I hadn't asked your mother the important question."

"To marry you," Tony said. "Romantic stuff again."

"A little. Don't sweat it," David said.

Meira had taken a sip of tea, but neither eating nor drinking held much appeal. "While your dad was working from his end, my father was trying to get us out of the country. I lobbied for us all to leave together, maybe to visit my brother in England, but Aba said that was too risky. If my mother went with me and they, the Popular Front, found out, she'd be at risk. And if we went to London, my brother could be in danger."

"They'd follow you there?"

"Aba was convinced the PFLP and Fatah had fairly sophisticated information-gathering operations, and he was in a position to know something about it. He planned to stay at my uncle's house, which was built like a fortress because my uncle's job was even more important than Aba's."

David said, "Once your mom and her family left for Tel Aviv, I figured my time was running out and I'd better get busy on that question."

"You proposed?"

"I did."

"Like on your knee in front of her?" The image must have amused Tony, because he relaxed enough to grin.

"Like on a bench on the boardwalk at sunrise," David said. "Much more comfortable, I can assure you."

"It was quite a spectacular morning," Meira said. "The sun sparkling on the Mediterranean made me forget for a moment all the mess surrounding us. So when your father took my hand and looked into my eyes, I saw the promise of love and protection. And I said yes."

"His eyes, huh? Boy, Dad, you had her fooled."

David raised his brow and punched Tony in the bicep. "Funny."

Tony's grin widened. "So, Mom, weren't you still scared?"

"Scared of your father?" she asked, smiling at their antics.

"You know, scared of the bad guys, scared to leave home. The whole thing."

When David had asked, her whole being had yearned toward him. And then reality had set in, the permanence of her decision, the yes that she'd uttered without conscious thought. "I was petrified. Especially because everyone seemed bent on making it happen immediately—the wedding and the leaving."

Yes, she'd wanted to be with David, but at what price? She hadn't had time to be certain of love, and suddenly everything had felt rushed.

And it had all been happening—had all become necessary—because she hadn't used the brains she'd been born with or the common sense her father had drilled into her. All because she'd presumed instead of relying on the training she'd received in the military when she'd been taught to look, to listen, and, above all, to be careful.

Instead, she'd fallen back into the pattern of her artistic self, her emotional, emotive self. And that choice had endangered every single person she loved.

She realized David was saying something. She tried to focus on words that sounded like "whisk her off to a faraway land." He rubbed his palms together in a gesture that used to make a younger Tony laugh.

At least it made him smile half-heartedly now.

She let a smile play on her face in response to Tony's effort as she picked up where she hoped David had stopped. "You were also planning to take me far from people who wanted to kill me."

"There was that." David set down his plate, looking at her with that old familiar gleam that set her heart beating in a little tap dance. "You seemed half in shock when we stood before the rabbi. All I could imagine was that you were marrying me because I was the lesser of two evils, and I felt desperate to show you how much I loved you. I wanted to distract you and talked about the grand adventure we were about to begin. I hated the thought of you being afraid. I wanted only to take care of you."

She sighed as his words sent a shiver through her that had nothing to do with fear. The darling man. "And I told you I wasn't so much afraid as I was furious. A madman was dictating our future, and we were running for our lives. Of course, I was furious."

The surprise in her son's eyes turned to a gleam that looked a lot like admiration. She laughed. David joined in. "You've never heard your mother act the warrior woman? Just wait until we get to the part in Virginia."

"Virginia?"

"You'll hear that soon enough. Right now, we need to tell you what happened at the airport on the day after our wedding."

"Our very small and intimate wedding in the hotel suite," Meira said. "Which was wonderful. But I suppose, being a guy, you'd rather hear about guns than weddings."

"Kinda."

∽

1979

The morning sky hid behind a translucent cloak of gray as a storm hovered offshore, forcing the sea into waves that it tossed at the beach. By afternoon, the wind would beat rain against the coastline from Haifa south.

They were supposed to leave that afternoon, but if planes couldn't take off once the weather worsened, Meira might be able to postpone her goodbyes. Another night and day here with her family would be lovely.

She'd hated it when Yaacov had left for school in England, but there'd always been the promise of him returning soon, of them together again, maybe not in the same house, but near enough to visit whenever they wished. Near enough for her to seek solace in her parents' love.

She couldn't believe she'd actually married a man from so far away. And yet, it might be the best and only way to protect her family from the repercussions of that one moment on the street when she'd been witness to a crime. Besides, she'd wanted to, hadn't she? For the first time in her life, she'd wanted to have it all with a man—home, family, children. If only she could have it all right here.

She packed quietly while David showered. He had little rearranging to do, other than to replace the suit he'd worn for the wedding with his traveling khakis.

When they joined her parents for a last breakfast, Ima grabbed her arms, drew her close, and whispered, "How was your wedding night? Good?"

Before she could answer her mother's question, David cleared his throat. "Meira, a little censorship."

His statement surprised an embarrassed bark of laughter from her. "Sorry. I got carried away." She grinned at her husband before turning back to their son. "Anyway, the storm blew itself out, and the flight was scheduled to leave as planned. The agony of departure hit me hard. Boarding a plane that would take me away from home and all I knew would have been impossible if your dad hadn't laced my fingers in his and reminded me that we were forever."

"Mush again, Dad," Tony said, obviously embarrassed.

"But it's G-rated mush. That's okay."

"So what happened next? Are you just going to talk about a boring old airplane ride?"

"Patience," David said.

Meira smiled. "Your grandparents went with us into the airport. Ima and Aba—my names for the ones you call Nonna and Nono."

"I guess all this is why I didn't get to call them Teta and Giddo, like Bahir's grandparents." He sounded resentful. "Because they're Jews."

Meira nodded, as if he'd spoken reasonably. Patience was the word of the day. "They liked the Latin version well enough, but it was hard having to avoid the truth when they visited us here. It nearly killed my Ima."

"It should've," Tony said, not quite under his breath.

Meira sucked in her breath, too stunned to reprimand him. That wasn't a problem for his father. "Don't let me *ever* hear you say something so ugly and cruel again."

Tony's head jerked up. His face had blanched. She was sure he'd never heard that harsh tone from his father. "I . . . I didn't mean . . ."

"Think, next time, before you open your mouth. You're not too old to find it washed with soap."

"Yes . . . yes, sir. I . . . I'm sorry, Mom. I didn't mean it."

"Your nonna loves you, Tony," she said. "Whatever name you use for her. And so do we."

He bit his lip and nodded, then swiped at tears with the heel of his hands.

"Now, let's get back to my story. You ready?"

Tony's head bobbed, but he didn't look at her.

"My parents went with us into the airport terminal. They planned to go straight from the airport to my uncle's house in Jerusalem."

1979

Meira wasn't certain why one particular movement caught her attention as she followed David toward the El Al desk. The terminal was crowded, people talking, hurrying, dragging suitcases. In spite of the chaos, she noticed a hand snaking out from under a jacket.

She was about to say something to David, but he must have also seen the hand and the gun it held, because he yanked her behind him.

It took mere seconds. As her husband whisked her out of the line of fire, an elderly Arab woman walked between them and the gunman, close enough for him to grab her and point his weapon at her head. She screamed.

The scream brought Meira peering around David's arm. It was the bomber, the knife wielder. People backed away.

"*Ya Elahi!*" The old woman babbled at the gunman in Arabic. "*Inta Majnoon!* You are crazy! Let me go!"

The madman pulled her with him as he backed against a nearby wall. He swung his gun in an arc before pointing it again at the old woman's head. "*Ikhrasi,* shut up!" he answered her in Arabic. Then he switched to Hebrew. "Don't anyone come too close, and you," he said to David, "you get out of the way, or I'll shoot this old lady and then both of you."

Aba raised himself to his full height and spoke with a haughty tone that was new to Meira. "You will not get away with this." He had moved in front of Ima.

When the old woman wouldn't stop squirming, the gunman tightened his hold until she squealed. "*Khalas!* Enough!" he said to her before turning back to Aba and then to David. "I will empty this gun before you or anyone can touch me." His voice was a low, vicious growl. "I will finish what we started. *Allahu Akbar!*"

Meira heard the threat. That crazed man would kill her new husband, and she could not let David sacrifice himself. She tried to step out from behind him, but he grabbed her wounded arm to keep her where she was. She cried out in pain.

"I'm sorry," he said over his shoulder. "Do *not* move."

She spoke to his back in low tones. "He will kill us both."

"He may kill me, but he'll be dead before he gets to you."

"And that's supposed to make me feel better?" She could be as adamant as he, but it did nothing for her temper or her fear.

FROM FIRE INTO FIRE

The crowd had parted, leaving her family, the gunman, and the elderly woman to stare at each other. Surely, though, there were other armed men in the airport. Someone would fix this.

And then she spotted a soldier signaling from behind his rifle, and her heartbeat accelerated. Hope surged as she willed the marksman to hurry. And to make his shot count before the gunman's trigger finger closed.

"Why didn't you just leave the country?" David asked the man. "You could have."

"Because of her," he said. "My brother at arms is even now being tortured in your jail. I know what happens. You Jews kill us. Therefore, I kill you. I am not afraid to die, but first I will take you—and her."

Lord, please do something.

"It doesn't have to end this way." David's grip tightened on the wrist he still held behind his back.

Did he want her to do something?

And then, as if at some signal she hadn't noticed, David dropped to the floor, dragging her down with him. She barely had time to register much before she heard the noise. When she looked up, she saw that a bullet had slammed into the gunman's head.

He had fallen, and it was ugly. It was very ugly.

"Oh, man. His head blew up?" Tony's eyes glittered with excitement.

Oops. She should have omitted that detail.

"Pretty gruesome," David told him. "But it was the fastest way to disarm him. That gun of his looked ready to go off into me or your mother."

"Did anyone throw up? I might have thrown up."

David shook his head. "I think they wanted to. Your mom and Nonna looked like they might, they were so pale, but there weren't many other people who saw the gore before someone covered him up."

"What'd they use? I mean, before the ambulance got there?"

"Somebody had a jacket. I didn't pay much attention because I was busy holding your mom. She couldn't stop shaking."

"So what happened then? He was dead and all, so wasn't that the end of things?"

"I wish," Meira answered.

╭╮

1979

A siren wailed outside the airport. David lifted her and cradled her to him. "I'm so sorry I was rough with you."

She could feel the thudding of his heart. As the blood rushed past her ears, she wondered if her own heartbeat were audible. Her mother's hands touched her hair, caressed her back. Her father's calm voice asked if they were okay.

"I hurt her," David said. "Trying to keep her from heroics."

Aba's laugh held no humor. "I saw that. Thank you. A little pain to her arm was a lot better than a bullet in her head."

Meira still couldn't speak. She might never speak again.

"He was a fool. Suicidal," David said, his attention focused on her.

A soldier approached her father. "Sir, are you all right?"

Aba nodded. "Thank you, son. I'm grateful for your presence."

"Yes, sir."

FROM FIRE INTO FIRE

David looked at her father. "You alerted them?"

"Your uncle did. We agreed it should be done, just in case someone wanted access to any of us."

Meira turned to her father and flung her good arm around his back. *"Toda, Aba. Toda raba."*

"Thank that marksman."

She dashed tears from her eyes. She felt suddenly exhausted.

"Come," David said. "I think we need to find somewhere to sit for a few minutes."

"No," she said. "First, we need to check into our flight."

David lifted her chin. "He's dead, you know. You don't have to rush to leave with me. If you want to stay here, you're free to do that, to take your time and follow me later."

They were safe, she and her family, at least as safe as anyone could be in a world where people hated them just because of their faith. She didn't have to go. Not today. Someday, yes, because she'd married him.

She hadn't had to do that either. And yet . . . and yet she had.

She looked into David's eyes and saw vulnerability. Taking his hand in hers, she stood on tiptoe to touch his lips with hers. "No. I don't have to go with you. But I want to."

The smile that spread across his features was so sweet, so welcoming, it made her want to spend the rest of her life basking in it.

"You're sure?" he asked.

"I am."

The bark of laughter from behind her and her father's whispered words broke the solemnity of the moment. "We chose well, my love, didn't we?"

"Hush, Eban," Ima answered. "We shouldn't gloat."

"But look at them. In love already."

Meira turned in David's arms to grin at her parents. "You chose very well."

⁂

"More mush," Tony said with all the disdain of an adolescent male.

"Absolutely," his father said. "Your mother's good at it."

Meira raised her brows. "And you're not?"

He winked at her. "Doing my humble best."

Tony slurped the remnants of his drink and rattled the ice cubes in his glass. Meira could see when his attitude shifted. He'd listened with curiosity to an exciting life-and-death story, but now he remembered why they were here.

"So," he said, the snark back in his voice, "a bad guy bit the dust. And you moved here."

"We're still at the beginning," David said.

"I don't think I want any more. I'm feeling kinda sick."

Maybe it was the soda. She could hope.

"We should take a break," Meira said, trying to salvage the moment and keep David's patience from thinning again. "Maybe get out of the house. You guys could take the canoe out. Or the sailboat."

"Nah. Can I just go lie down?"

"A nap sounds like a great alternative." Meira stood and gathered their glasses. "Maybe we'll order pizza tonight. Find a good movie."

"Sure," Tony said, but his shuffling feet didn't bode well for an evening of forgetfulness.

When his bedroom door closed behind him, she turned to her husband. "This isn't going well."

"Maybe, maybe not. We knew it would be hard."

"Remind me again why we waited so long?"

"Picture him hanging out with Bahir and casually mentioning that his mother and father are spies. Were you thinking show and tell in school?"

Meira combed her hair back with her fingers. "I know. And if he'd known and been forced to silence, it would have killed him. And if we'd had to send him away earlier, it might have killed me. He's still such a boy."

"I don't think secrets are part of the vocabulary of a kid. Even for an almost fourteen-year-old."

"That's the part that's going to be the hardest, isn't it?" she said. "The fact that he won't be able to tell Bahir. Or visit his best friend again. It'll be like a death."

"Let's just hope the psychology books are right and that kids are resilient."

"Maybe they are to things that can't be helped. I'm not so sure about disillusionment. Not when we could have chosen differently."

9 Tony

He pulled down the shades to darken his room, kicked off his sneakers, and flung himself on his bed. He'd quit naps about a zillion years ago, but he'd had to get out of there. Not to sleep. Just to quiet the buzzing in his head.

The ceiling fan whirred overhead, its blades circling round and round. Staring at the twirling motion started to hurt his eyes. He threw his arm across his forehead.

It wasn't fair. He should be on the beach with Bahir instead of stuck here.

He had to admit his parents' story was kind of interesting, all those guns, bad guys, and a superhero marksman saving his mom.

Maybe that part was true, and maybe they'd made it up to give themselves a reason for lying. Lying was wrong, no matter how you cut it, and to your *kid*?

Come to think of it, when he was five, maybe six, he'd said he didn't have any candy hidden under his covers. That had been a lie, because he'd been sucking on some lollipops his nonna had brought and put in the pantry for special occasions. Anyhow, his mom had known he was fibbing, and she and Dad had taken him into the living room to have a talk, how they said he was supposed to tell the truth. No matter what.

He'd brought out the candy he'd sneaked, and then he had to listen to them talk about sneaking and taking. They'd told him lying was something forbidden by God. Had they meant Allah? Maybe Allah hated lying, but the Jewish God—what did they call him? HaShem?—didn't seem to care so much. Because they were Jews, and they lied.

But if they were Jews, he was, too.

His head started to pound, as if one of those little hammers like the one his dad used for hanging pictures was in there, pinging away at his skull.

Who was he supposed to believe?

A mom and dad who told him never to lie or a mom and dad who lied?

10   Meira

She carried a tray with a couple of slices of triple-cheese pizza into Tony's room and set it on his desk. "Here you go. In case you change your mind and feel hungry."

He lay curled toward the wall. She waited a moment to see if he'd give her a chance to say more or if he'd speak, but he remained silent, unmoving, and she retreated to the living room where she and David nibbled a little and sipped wine and pretended to read.

Crickets began a serenade. An owl hooted. Dogs barked somewhere across the lake.

It had begun to cool by the time they heard Tony pad down the hall to the bathroom. The toilet flushed, and water whooshed through the old pipes. He headed back to bed, and his light went off. They barely spoke as they switched off the living room lamps, carried their glasses to the kitchen sink, and retreated to their own room.

They shared a prayer, this one laced with pleas for peace, for HaShem to touch their son and bless him. A single peck to the lips, and David turned away. She fluffed her pillow under her head and stared into the dark.

She shut her eyes, barely moving as sleep hid from her. David tossed off the top sheet and soon pulled it back up. She knew each time he turned as she lay there, listening, hoping, praying. For hours.

What could they have done differently? What else could they have done twelve years ago? Or even five years or three years ago?

What about yesterday?

"What are you thinking?" David's voice came from the darkness, husky with exhaustion.

"Nothing, everything."

"Worrying?"

"How can I not? Were we wrong to have begun this thing?"

He sighed and sat up, propping pillows at his back. Then he tugged her up to his chest. "I don't know."

The moon had risen, and its glow illuminated them. Full moons meant the promise of something, but they tugged at her heart. There'd been a full moon at their beginning, hadn't there? All those long years ago.

"It all started in Jerusalem, didn't it? I mean, once I'd identified that man and we'd come here . . ."

He traced a finger across her bare shoulder and down the thin strap of her gown. "Do you remember when I proposed to you?"

She sat upright, a laugh choked out of her. "Are you trying

to distract me?"

"Maybe. But I was lying here, going back over the years and the choices we made. I'm not sure I had a choice once I lifted you from the road that day and carried you to the car."

"Really?"

"You caught me. And with all that followed, the door to love opened, and I walked right in."

"The sun shone the day you proposed. I remember how bright it was."

"It glittered off your hair. I was surprised by the color."

She turned toward him. "You hadn't noticed before?"

"I suppose I'd never seen it with sunlight hitting at that angle. You have red in it."

"Well, yes."

"I was petrified you'd say no. It was too soon."

She sighed and settled back against his chest. "Much too soon."

"But you said yes."

"Well, you were very attractive. And your eyes, so blue. I thought the laugh lines at their corners must mean you enjoyed life." She trailed her fingers up his chest to his neck, tracing the line of his jaw. "Besides, you promised me adventure."

That surprised a guffaw from him. "But you didn't want adventure. You wanted peace. And to stay home."

"That's true, but marrying you seemed like a good idea at the time."

He lifted her off him and brought her up for a peck on her lips. "Your memory has been clouded. You thought it horrifying."

Pulling herself free, she straddled his legs so she could peer at him. She could just make out his features. "Only in the abstract. Leaving home, not knowing you, traveling so far away, getting *married*, which meant forever in my book. Those frightened me." Then she leaned close to his face. "But in the concrete, the immediate, there was this gorgeous man who made me feel things I'd never imagined, whose smile nearly knocked me over, and who seemed to have fallen for me." She moved closer still. Her voice became a whisper. "Besides, he had great taste in rings."

"You sold yourself for diamonds and sapphires?" he whispered back.

"And a hard body."

"And you knew that how?"

"Honey, you carried me. I was very close to those muscles."

"You liked my body?"

"Even before I met it skin to skin."

She braced her hands on his shoulders and closed the distance between their lips until hers brushed lightly against his. And then he cupped her face in his hands and deepened that kiss until they didn't think or worry about anything else but bodies and touches and kisses and loving.

Drugged with pleasure, she ignored morning until David set a steaming mug on the bedside table and kissed her forehead. "I'm going for a run. He hasn't come out of his room."

"Thank you for the coffee." She pulled the pillow over her head. She wasn't ready to face the day, and running sounded like torture.

She finally climbed from bed and padded into the bathroom. As she brushed her teeth, she stared at the haggard face purporting to be hers.

It couldn't be. Those were lines. That was a sag at her neck.

A shower didn't help. It certainly didn't erase lines or sags. She towel-dried her hair, pulled on shorts and a tee shirt, and took her cold coffee to the kitchen where she brewed another pot. While it dripped, she wandered to the lakeside window and stared out at the water.

Her son sat hunched at the end of the dock with his knees drawn up. At the sight of his wet hair, her heart did a somersault. He'd gone swimming. Alone.

He was never supposed to go in the water alone. None of them swam alone. The prospect of what could have happened terrified her.

What had they done?

She heard the slap of shoes on the steps as David climbed to the porch. She intercepted him, but all she could do was point.

He barely paused before turning and jogging back down the steps and toward the dock. Tony didn't look up as his father approached. David lowered himself beside his son.

When the coffee pot had filled, she poured herself a cup, added cream and sugar, and set about making pancakes. She had a batch in the oven keeping warm when her men trooped inside.

She looked through the open doorway. David shook his head, so she kept her questions to herself. "Pancakes?"

With his hand on Tony's shoulder, her husband smiled. "Lovely. Do I have time for a quick shower?"

"Tony? You ready for some?"

"In a sec." He headed to his room, to change clothes, she assumed.

"Five minutes," her husband called.

It killed her not to ask questions, to wait until they sat. David bowed his head and spoke a prayer, invoking Adonai's help and blessings.

Tony sat, stone-faced, staring at his plate.

Her boy's anger hurt. It felt like a knife slicing her open for a slow bleed-out.

"You don't have to agree with our faith," his father said, "but you do have to show respect and courtesy."

"Why? Did you show it to me when you lied? And who is this God of yours if he lets you lie?"

"There's a difference between lying and omitting facts," David said. "We allowed you to believe certain things because your belief in them would protect you."

"And you," Tony said, pouting.

"And our mission."

"Which was to lie."

Meira set down her fork. "No. Our mission was to ferret out bits of information to help stop terrorists—like the one who killed all those people in Jerusalem that day. The one who tried to kill me."

Tony didn't respond, nor did his facial expression soften.

She turned to her husband. "I think we should tell him what happened in Virginia."

"Virginia?" Tony asked. "What happened there?"

"You eat. Then we'll tell you."

After Tony had washed the breakfast dishes, Meira led the way back to the living room. She eased down onto one of the chairs and decided she ought to recover them. The place would need brightening once they'd finished baring their souls, something lighter on the cushions after they'd absorbed all the heaviness of confession and tears.

David sat and started the story. "When I married your mother, I had an engineering job in a place called Newport News, Virginia. By the time you came along, we'd bought a little house in a rural community across the peninsula. You were a baby, not quite a year, when this part of the story took place."

"I lived in Virginia?" Tony sounded incredulous. "I was born there?"

"You were."

"How come I never knew?"

"Because our life and our names changed after that. The story gets rather involved here, and I'll let your mother begin."

11 Meira

1983

Meira's dried-up creative juices were sucking the soul out of her. She adored her husband and her sweet baby boy whose blue eyes were so like his father's. She loved their quaint cottage next to the river with its garden, its view, and her art studio. The space was perfect. Or at least it was when her eyes and her hands coordinated with her mind to fill an empty canvas.

While her son napped in the next room, she sat in the spare bedroom, staring again at the easel and a blank canvas. Charcoal pencils lay on the table next to her with an unopened drawing tablet on the floor nearby.

She lined up her brushes and set her pencils carefully back in their case. She knew David was worried about work. His commute to the shipyard took less than half an hour, but his work hours had been extended after a group in Texas bought the yard and started reorganizing. His immediate superior had even brought in a nephew who coveted David's job, and her normally placid husband feared his position would hit the chopping block of that nephew's ambition.

Did worrying about David explain her own inability to create?

No. She'd always created. Always, even during her military service. Her sketches from those years had turned into watercolors once she returned home.

And now? Nothing. Her muse had dried up until it seemed prune-like: wrinkled, unpalatable.

David said it was fatigue from taking care of the baby, but Tony was an easy child. His early bouts with colic had ended at around six months. He ate well. And he could pull himself up and walk holding on to the furniture. He was only days away from independent steps. Yes, he was teething, but that wasn't a new experience.

A ringing phone took her to the kitchen. She lifted the receiver to hear David's voice. "Hey, babe. Tony napping? You busy?"

"Well . . ."

"Still having trouble?"

"Mmm." She wished he wouldn't ask, but perversely would probably resent it if he didn't.

"Can you handle company tonight for dinner?" He sounded apologetic, as if she'd mind a grown-up distraction. If he only knew how welcome that sounded.

"Of course. Who?"

"It's the strangest thing. I just got off the phone with a

cousin of mine, a man I don't even know, except by reputation."

"Reputation?"

"He's my mother's cousin. I've heard his name mentioned by my Uncle Avram." He cleared his throat.

"And?"

"And he works in intelligence."

"Oh." With effort, she kept her tone light. "Is he here on pleasure or for work?"

"He said he'll tell us tonight."

No one said things like that if they brought good news. She tried to sound positive and to make herself feel it. "Can you pick up fresh fish? Maybe grill them?"

"Sure. Anything else?"

"I can manage the rest."

"You'll be busy with the baby. Why don't I stop at the deli here in town and grab a few things to go with fish?"

"Oh, David, that would be great. I have salad fixings, but if you do the rest, I'd be grateful. And now your heir is stirring."

She had time to put herself and Tony together and straighten the living areas. They could serve a Pinot Grigio. Or should it be beer? David would like wine, and they had a lovely bottle he'd brought home last week. She had no idea what his cousin drank.

This would be good, her husband having family come. When a small-plane crash had robbed him of his parents, it had been months before he'd stopped staring blankly at walls or out windows.

He'd taken time off to deal with their estate and sell their Florida condo. She may not have known the senior Rassadims for long, but she'd known them well enough to mourn with

David and to grieve for the hole this loss left in their life, a hole her own family could only fill on occasion, thanks to the miles that separated them.

Distance. She hated it. She missed community, which they hadn't yet found here in Virginia. The people were friendly enough, but they had their own circle of friends with whom they shared history and interests. Most were churchgoers who attended either the Methodist church in town or the Episcopal one a little farther out in the country. The closest synagogue was about forty minutes away in Newport News, and the distance didn't help with friend making.

Perhaps it hadn't been such a great idea to buy in a rural area, but she hadn't known any better, and neither had David. How could she have, when all she'd known had been a nation filled with family, with those who understood her past if not always her present? Sometimes when she visited a local shop, conversation stopped as if people here didn't know what to do with this stranger from Israel, this Jewish artist trying to find her way among the wives of fisherman and farmers. She missed, with an almost inconsolable ache, having Ima around. Ima adored her grandson, and Meira needed her mother's reassurance that she could manage this rearing-a-child thing. That's what mothers did for their daughters, wasn't it?

Maybe that's why she couldn't create. Insecurity. Worry. Loneliness.

Tony nuzzled her when she lifted him from the crib. The sweet scent of his hair made her heart constrict. Before this baby, she'd never known what mother-love meant, that soul-wrenching, all-enveloping love that could bring tears to her eyes just from looking at him.

She changed him, cooing, tickling his fat stomach, loving it when he rewarded her with a gurgle of glee. And then, while she tried to secure the dry diaper, he let loose, soaking the dry one with pee. She'd learned early on to take care so he didn't douse her, and this time only the new diaper got drenched. "Thank you so much, boy-o."

He continued to grin and chortle as she fastened him into yet another diaper and pulled on another pair of overalls.

In the kitchen, she plopped him in his highchair, gave him a plastic sippy cup of juice, and peeled some apple sections to tide him over while she worked. He chatted in baby talk and ate and showed off his few teeth. And he drooled, which was what he did when he had another one coming in.

She would not think of their guest's reasons for visiting as she set the table with multicolored woven placemats they'd picked up during a visit to Portsmouth, added cloth napkins and cutlery, and set about washing the lettuce and slicing tomatoes. The baby opened and closed his fat little fist. Concentrating only on him and the movement of her knife, she diced a tomato section and added the small chunks to his tray.

Sweet baby. Sweet innocent.

"That good, kiddo?" she asked when he stuffed them in his cheeks. "Chew now. That's it."

He kept busy with tomato bits while she fluffed up pillows and dusted the end tables.

She was wiping Tony's face and hands when she heard the front door open and David call her name.

"In here," she answered, lifting Tony from his high chair. His legs kicked against her sides as if she were a pony he wanted to hurry along. That boy loved his daddy.

David took his son and leaned in to kiss her cheek. Tony

planted his palms on each side of David's face to draw the attention his way. "You want yours, too, big boy?" David asked, planting a loud smooch on the baby's lips. Tony giggled.

"Honey," David said, turning toward the living room, "here's our guest, Eli Rosen."

"Shalom," she said in welcome.

Eli stood almost as tall as David, but he was thin where her husband had muscles. David enjoyed exercise, and she guessed Eli preferred a seat behind a desk and that he'd been occupying it for a while now.

They spoke pleasantries in Hebrew, and Eli helped David with the grill while Tony supervised from his playpen and she sorted the deli food onto platters.

Tony, happy with his audience and the finger food they put on his high-chair tray during dinner, made it all the way to seven o'clock before the fussies set in. She got him settled for the night while David cleaned up.

When she joined the men, they were seated on the front porch, enjoying the cool breeze off the river. David handed her a glass of wine.

"Great looking boy you have," Eli said.

"Thank you." She wondered when he'd get to the point of his visit.

"I was telling David that I met his father years ago, when he visited Israel to carry my cousin away with him. A fine man. He'd have loved watching that boy of yours grow up."

"Yes, he would have." Meira spoke to spare David.

"I'm glad your parents can visit you."

"Yes. I am, too." Enough of this, Meira decided. "I doubt you came all the way here to talk about family."

The way Eli cleared his throat and then leaned forward, resting one forearm across his knees, made Meira want to retreat to the kitchen. Or ask him to leave.

"You're right, but can we talk out here?"

"Why wouldn't we be able to?" Meira asked. Their neighbors were exactly in chatting distance, and a hedge separated the driveways. She didn't imagine anyone had come out to eavesdrop.

Eli glanced around, then scooted his chair in closer. "We will speak in Hebrew," he said, shifting to that language.

It felt very cloak and dagger. "Fine," she said, growing more curious by the moment.

"We recently picked up a member of the Popular Front who carried a list of names in his pocket. One was yours, Meira." Eli paused, whether for effect or just to make sure they listened, she didn't know. "Your married name."

His words seemed to suck the breath out of her. "How? How could they have found it? Have they traced us here?"

"We cannot be certain, but we did receive intel that there are operatives in place in this country. Whether or not one is actually in Virginia, I do not know."

"Could they have followed you?" Her voice rose. She heard it slide into panic.

"I wish I could answer that," Eli said, lowering his own voice in response.

David stood as if the threat had shot him from the chair. And then he braced himself against the porch railing. "Why?" he asked over his shoulder. "Why do they still want her?"

Eli shrugged. "Vengeance?"

"You mean, because she saw a face and identified a murderer? He was killed because he'd killed, because he was trying to kill again. Why didn't it end there?"

"And," Meira asked, "why only now? It's been over three years. What took them so long?"

"If it is the killer's cousin Abreeq Husseini spearheading the effort, he only recently got out of jail again."

"Again?" Meira said.

"This time for brandishing a knife at a soldier. He did not actually attack anyone, or he would still be locked up." Eli sighed and rubbed a hand across his forehead. "I do not pretend to understand the minds of madmen. But that is what we are dealing with, madmen who hate and who believe in the law of retaliation. In their mind, you caused one of them to die, so the law of retaliation would allow—or even compel— his family to come against you."

"And my parents?" She almost whispered the words. "My brother?"

"They have been alerted, but your father thinks they are safe enough."

"How? If I'm not, they're not."

Meira glanced toward the door. Her baby. No one would touch her baby.

"Their move to a condo that is not listed in their name gives us reason to believe they are relatively secure. The building is monitored and guarded. The same for your brother."

"And someone else lives in my childhood home."

He nodded. She had known when her father sold their house as a precaution, to help keep Ima safe. She'd known and wept, realizing once again that a moment out of time, when she'd witnessed something she wasn't supposed to see, had wreaked havoc for her entire family.

David moved to stand behind her chair, his hands on her shoulders. "I'm sure you didn't come here just to tell us this. After all, a letter would have sufficed. Or a phone call. What else is on your mind?"

Eli cleared his throat as if he were trying to dislodge more than phlegm. In the dim lighting, Meira saw him steeple his fingers in front of his lips, then lower them so he could be heard. "You both know, do you not, about the mess Lebanon has become?"

Every newscast from Beirut revealed the destruction of what had been called the Paris of the Middle East. Once upon a time, her father had taken them by way of an aerial tramway to a beautiful restaurant on the hills overlooking the Mediterranean Sea. From that vantage point, the sea near shore had appeared a light turquoise, darkening to cobalt as it deepened. A stream meandered next to the restaurant with a couple of swans, maybe a duck or two, paddling around. There'd been *mezza*, the small dishes served with the *arak* her father'd accepted from their Lebanese hosts. Aba had said the drink tasted like licorice, but it turned a milky white when poured over ice.

Beirut had seemed so European, and Meira's heart broke to imagine the civil war's devastation. Syrians had added their might to the other Islamic militants who wanted to wrest control from any who supported the former accommodation leadership that had included Maroni Christians in key government positions. The compromise government, which had existed since the French left after WWII, had drawn wealth and Western culture to what had been an enclave of sophistication. The tensions between the Christians and the Muslims had always existed, but after Al Fatah and other radical Palestinian groups moved in, they'd stirred tensions by riling the poor, especially the Shia who felt disenfranchised by both the Christians and the Sunni majority. How sad that Beirut had fallen victim to these radicals. And here they were now, with the UN involved and the future looking dismal for that once lovely country.

"What does Lebanon have to do with us?" David drew his chair next to Meira's and sat close enough to take her hand. "With my need to protect Meira and our son?"

"I am coming to that," Eli said. "The Palestinian guerrillas are shelling Israel from southern Lebanon, drawing us into a nasty conflict that continues to intensify. The UN is useless, and we have had to defend ourselves in the world's court of public opinion, while former allies within the U.S. wage another kind of war to discredit us. Fortunately, there are other factions here who support Israel."

"I've been a little out of that end of things," David said. "Busy, you know. Living." He coughed slightly. "Here."

Eli fiddled with a cigarette, but he didn't light it. "We need all the help we can get."

"What do you mean by 'help'? Because it looks like we have a few needs at our end."

She let David talk. All she wanted was to show this bearer of bad news to his rental car. To go inside and hold her little boy close and never let him go. To make herself and her family invisible to terrorists.

"I do not think your needs and ours are mutually exclusive." Eli spoke with an oily serpent's voice. "When things settle down, we are going to need eyes on the ground, those who can help us by fitting into the culture in a casual way."

"Again, what's that got to do with us?" David sounded surprised.

She willed him to snarl at that man who was quickly becoming her own personal public enemy number two—directly in line after the terrorist, or terrorists, who still had her in their sights. She was a wife. A mother. Who now had to deal with hiding—and possibly running—from danger again. She was not going to listen to some do-gooder try to push his probably dangerous agenda on her too nice—and therefore gullible—husband.

The interfering Eli continued to talk. "We have been formulating a different methodology for informal information-gathering over the last few years, some of it based on a task force put together by your father, Meira. Trained assets are needed everywhere to protect our small country from the hostile forces surrounding us, and ears on every piece of ground are hard to maintain."

Her father's task force? The one he'd been working on when she and David had fled? Eli's words felt like ice water pouring over her. She shivered.

Stop, she wanted to say. Just stop. Go away.

"So, you're what?" David said, "Asking me—us—to join this fight? Sign up with Mossad or some other agency of yours?" His voice hit a higher note on that last question. She cheered him on with the nod of her head, but she clamped her jaw closed against words she wasn't ready to voice. He paused, and the quiet settled momentarily. When he spoke, he'd regained control. "Look, we have a one-year-old son, and in case you hadn't noticed, this is our home. A-me-ri-ca."

"But your home and your security are now at risk. You need to hide, and I can offer you a way to do that. Besides, your children will have a stake in Israel's future—as your extended family does now. Israel is our homeland."

She squeezed David's hand. In the light from the lamp at the back of the house, she saw his frown. And then he slapped at a mosquito, and the frown deepened.

The breeze had stilled, bringing the nasty bugs out. "We should head inside," he said. "We will listen, but only that."

They stood, moved the chairs out of the way, and headed into the living room, silent on the subject until they were settled, and Meira had replaced wine glasses with water.

"Hiding from this latest threat to your family will require another name change and a move," Eli said, switching back to English. "If you help us, we can facilitate that. We aren't suggesting anything dangerous for you, but rather something that will allow you to hide in plain sight."

"In Lebanon?" Meira asked.

"Eventually."

Tony voice cut into the story. "I don't like that guy."

"Eli?" his father asked.

"Yeah. He just wanted to use you and Mom. He didn't care about me. And I was just a little kid."

"I think he did care, but he had a bigger picture in mind."

"What, like world peace?" Tony asked with a sneer.

Meira smiled, ignoring the sneer and the sarcasm. "A lot like world peace."

"So he made you guys into liars."

"No, what happened next accomplished that," David said.

12 DAVID

1983

Trouble loomed. David felt his wife's silence weighting the air around him like a fog so moisture-laden he could barely breathe. Her knuckles rose against his touch as her fingers curled in her lap.

While this cousin of his droned on, David tried to listen, to give the man a chance to be heard. Eli spoke of people dying—their people—which was bad enough. But then he used the word *courage*. David resented anyone who resorted to emotional manipulation, and Eli's performance could win him an Oscar.

"Think how many lives could be saved if enough people provided correct and timely intelligence. If we knew what the enemy planned before they executed it." Eli continued playing dirty by reminding them of the roles a few good people had played during WWII in trying to save Jewish lives. He claimed he was giving them an opportunity to do what they were both good at: befriending people of all nationalities and listening for clues that could help save lives.

"Working with us shouldn't put you in any danger or anywhere near actual terrorists," Eli said. "And if one did cross your path, he wouldn't know you were working against him. Snatches of conversations or gossip could point us in the right direction. You wouldn't have to do more than that. If you see or hear something suspicious, we'd send in men trained to take care of it."

David sighed. "You have other folk doing this sort of thing?"

"We've already had people send us gossip from a couple of countries, and we've used it to stop a car bombing and an assassination."

"Oh, my," Meira said.

Still skeptical, David asked, "Why us?"

"You're a logical choice. Avram approached me after he and Meira's father spoke. Once they'd discovered your name on that list."

"Wait," Meira said. "My father knows you're here?"

"He does. He wanted to be the one to approach you, but we couldn't risk a phone call, and he couldn't get away to travel. Besides, that might have alerted the wrong people. They picked me because of our family relationship and the fact that no one knows my real job, which meant I wasn't likely to rouse suspicions."

"But why do you want to enlist us?" Meira asked. "Why would my father suggest it?"

"Your father's worried about this new threat on your life, which means a threat to his grandson as well. If someone is actually in this country looking for you, your lives could be in imminent danger, requiring immediate and radical changes for your protection. We all felt we could offer you greater protection and opportunity than anything you could manage on your own."

"But becoming *spies*?" she asked. "How does that protect us? Especially Tony? He's a baby. He'll be a child."

David heard the fear in her voice and almost called a halt to the discussion. Meira didn't need anything else to stoke the tension she'd carried for months. If he guessed right, the tension was what had shut down her ability to paint, and the only time peace stilled her jitters seemed to be when she lay with him in bed or when she cuddled their son close to her breast. He was convinced her moodiness came from her isolated existence in this house, so far from home and family.

Now, this new danger had dropped on them, another wedge between her and her home in Israel, between her and tranquility. But what Eli suggested wouldn't bring her closer to them. Instead, it would isolate her further.

Eli raised his hands, palms toward them. "Meira, take a deep breath—"

David recoiled, because his wife *hated* anyone telling her to relax. "It's not just Meira," he said. "And I don't know how you expect us to relax when you talk about sending us into enemy territory."

"I apologize, but you wouldn't be spies in the traditional sense. I mean, no one's asking you to go all 007 on us."

What? Did his cousin think this was the time for humor? Before David could speak, Meira said, "A spy is a spy is a spy. He has to tell lies and pretend to be someone he isn't so he can gain knowledge that wouldn't otherwise be available to him. I don't care what pretty wrapping you put on it, that's spying." She paused for only a moment. "Just why would we want to do that?"

Tony gave her a high five, bringing her back to the present. "That's telling him, Mom. But how come you didn't just make him go away?" He squinted at David. "What about you? Did you give him what-for?"

David laughed. "I did my best. But there was a lot riding on our decision. Like your safety. And your mother's."

1983

David longed to tell Eli to go away and leave them to figure out how to protect themselves and Tony. If they agreed to this charade Eli had suggested, they'd have to deny, at least publicly, the generational, social, and religious tie to that preeminent relationship—their Jewishness.

When Eli spoke again, he said, "It's only a matter of time before the Popular Front or its cohorts find out more than your married name. You're fluent in Arabic as well as English, French, and Hebrew, and, from what I understand, David's always been a whiz at languages. You're a perfect fit for the program. As an American, David won't be expected to have the same proficiency you do, Meira."

"But they hate Americans," she said.

David agreed. And the idea of learning Arabic while also trying to earn a living sounded just oh-so-fun. "Arabic has a different alphabet. A completely different alphabet."

"You speak Hebrew," Eli said, "and many words are the same. You'll pick it up easily enough. And the people we're talking about don't hate Arab-Americans. As a matter of fact, they recruit people from the States and try to lure them away from the liberal way of life and the trappings of Western civilization. If you're willing to help us, there are a few things that we'll need to put in place soon."

The logistics seemed overwhelming. Granted, they needed to get out of the line of fire of any crazies who made it across the Atlantic. But Lebanon? David shook his head. "Lebanon isn't a place I want to visit, much less take a baby. This just won't work for us."

Eli held out his hand to stop the words. "No one wants to send you in while the civil war rages, but it won't last forever. We're thinking years down the road. Years for you to prepare. All we'd need from you at this point is a willingness to begin the process. We can use you in the States once things are in place."

"What does 'begin the process' mean?" Meira asked. "What would you want from us?"

"Submit to a name change, a relocation."

"Explain," David said.

"If you agree to help, we'll supply you with new passports, a new job, a language tutor, and a home in another city. You would become Da'oud and Mirah Rasad." He spelled Meira's Arabic name.

David wondered how much the death of his parents had influenced Avram's choice when he'd sent Eli here. "Was

Meira's safety the only reason you picked us? Or did it have anything to do with my having no family left outside of Israel?"

Eli shrugged. "I'm sure that weighed in the discussions. But the main issue is the safety of your entire family. Our solution takes care of that."

"Maybe in the short term," Meira said, "but how would we get back into Israel? How would I visit my parents?"

"Any way we look at this, there are going to be difficulties and compromises. You're no longer safe as Meira and David Rassadim. But as Da'oud and Mirah Rasad, you'd have freedom of movement. The logistics could be managed, just as your father managed their living arrangements."

David stood abruptly and paced to the patio's edge before turning to glare at his cousin. "There's bound to be some law about impersonating someone—and if there isn't, there should be—and there's bound to be one that forbids U.S. citizens from working for a foreign country."

Eli's chuckle sounded smug. "Well, no. The only issue would be if you worked against U.S. interests or involved yourself in a conflict against the United States. The faction in your government I mentioned earlier? There are people at the highest levels who want a safe Middle East in which the Jewish homeland can prosper and survive, and they have approved this program."

"You've got to be kidding me," David said.

"What can I say? Except to note that they've promised to cover those who are part of this ultra-secret program."

David looked over at Meira, whose squint probably matched his, although he couldn't see it in the dim light. "Do you trust them?" she asked him.

"About as far as I can spit," David said.

"That's what I'm thinking."

Eli cleared his throat. "If they fail to protect you, we will."

"If you could protect us, we wouldn't be having this discussion," David said.

Meira stood. "Eli, may I get you anything else before we call it a night?"

"No, thank you. I know you're tired, as I am. Perhaps you will think about my proposal?"

David nodded. "We'll promise to consider it. Now, do you think you'll be able to find your way back to your hotel in the dark?"

"I should. You want to go over the turns I'll have to make before I get to a highway?"

"It'll be easier if I just lead you out to the main road," David said, grabbing his keys off the entry table. "Once you're on it, you won't have any trouble getting to the interstate and your exit."

"I would be very grateful." He turned to Meira. "Thank you so much for your hospitality. We will speak again."

"*Bivakasha*," Meira said. "You're welcome."

David leaned in to kiss her. "Be right back."

They'd resolved nothing. Yes, they needed to hide. But to head into danger, even if that danger were years away?

They were getting ready for bed when Tony woke, fussing. "I'll get him," Meira said. "It's probably that tooth."

"You need help?"

"I'll give him something if he has a fever and rock him until he settles."

Rocking their snuggly boy helped settle his parents, too. If

Tony woke later, David would take a turn. After all, it was only fair that he get in some baby time.

Before long, he heard Meira's sweet voice singing a lullaby, and he smiled to himself.

When the phone rang, he reached across the bed to grab the receiver and listened while Eli spoke. Then he walked into the baby's room.

"Eli thinks someone may have followed him to his hotel."

13 Tony

His dad stood. "I need a break. And food."

Tony's mouth fell open. "You can't quit. Not *there*. Not with a bad guy showing up."

Mom headed toward the hall. "First dibs on the bathroom."

Dad laughed. "I'll go forage. Cheese okay?"

"That works," she said over her shoulder. "Don't forget the pickles."

Tony's stomach rumbled at the mention of food. Fine, if he had to wait for answers, he'd eat.

"Come help spread the bread." Dad waved him toward the kitchen.

"It's not fair. You know the ending. I mean, I get it. You're alive, but did you get shot at? Were there guns?"

"Food first," his dad said. "Patience."

Patience. Great. He *hated* someone telling him that, like he could just will himself not to want answers or to wait for something.

What about that Eli person? Was he dead?

Nah. He seemed like the sorta guy who got other people killed. Not himself.

See, there were too many questions. If these Popular Front guys were Palestinians, that made them Arabs. Arabs, like Bahir and his family. Like the kids in school. Like his teachers. And Mr. Munir at the grocery. And what about Mr. Faisal, who took care of their building? Or Wafa and Madg, Mr. Faisal's daughters?

Tony's *friends*.

He knew there were bad guys and good guys everywhere, but not like this. His friends in Lebanon would never try to kill his mom and dad just because his mom had seen something that got a bad guy shot.

Maybe the PFLP was like the mob. The Mafia was a bunch of Italians who killed people, but not all Italians were in the mob, and not all were bad.

Okay. That made sense. A few bad guys gave the rest a bad name.

Only, how come his parents didn't get that?

He dipped the spreading knife into the mayo. He and his mom liked mayo and mustard. His dad only liked mustard. He slathered some on the bread his dad had put on the plates, one slice and then the next.

"Dad, are you gonna keep lying to Dr. Ramah and his wife?"

"Bahir's parents?" His father opened a jar of pickles and

started slicing them. "Why don't we talk about that after you've heard the whole story? Can we do that?"

"It's not right. You won't say, so that means you're gonna."

"It means we'll talk about it later. Put cheese on one side of the bread while I get the lettuce washed."

"Dr. Ramah is your friend."

"I know. He's a good man."

"But you don't trust him."

"It's not that. Nasri and Hala are good people who hate evil and violence as much as we do."

Mom walked in, and he could tell she'd heard because she took the lettuce from dad and didn't say anything.

"Mom, you hang out with Mrs. Ramah. How can you do that and look her in the face, saying you're somebody you're not?"

She turned and leaned her back against the counter. "It's not spoken, honey. I don't stand there and lie to her face. Yes, she assumes things about me that aren't true, and I don't fix that…"

Suddenly, her eyes looked really sad and a little scared, and her sigh was loud. "Maybe we've asked too much of you. Maybe we shouldn't have assumed you were old enough to understand."

He stared at her. What did she mean? She wished they'd kept on lying to him? "You think you shouldn't have told me yet?" His voice hit a high note and made a squeak, but he didn't care.

"No, of course not. I'm just worrying out loud."

"I'm old enough to know the truth. I always was."

"Oh, sweetie. Try to trust us, will you?"

Yeah, easy for her to say. But right now? Hard to do. Really hard to do.

Going along with them would destroy his whole life.

14 Meira

1983

Had someone actually followed Eli, or was that a spy's overactive imagination at work? David hadn't seen anything out of the ordinary when he'd led Eli out of town.

"Stay in here, will you," he asked her. "Try to keep the baby calm and quiet?"

"What about you? What are you going to do?"

"Check the locks and turn out the inside lights. I'll make sure the outside's illuminated, but that leaves the sides of the house vulnerable, so stay away from the windows—even if it's dark in here."

"Your gun?"

The idea that they might need a gun here in rural Virginia appalled her. Yes, they'd followed her father's advice that they both be armed, but the pistols were locked away, untouched except when they went to the range once a week to keep their skills honed.

"I'm getting them both. You need yours at the ready, too."

"Oh, David." This was just too much. Why was it happening now, and why here? She wished she could blame David's cousin for leading someone to the house. "What will Eli do?"

"Call it in, but if he follows the chain of command, that's a lot of people between him and any help for us."

So they'd sit here, waiting for something to happen? That sounded worse than risking a departure. "Why don't we go to a motel?"

"If anyone's out there, we'd be more vulnerable than if we stay here."

"I wish it were daylight."

David looked at his watch. "It will be in about seven hours."

"Thanks." Seven hours to worry and watch and wait. She looked down at her sleeping son. "I'll put him back in bed and watch over him."

"Be right back."

She listened to her husband's footsteps move through the house as he checked windows and doors. When he returned, he set her revolver along with a box of ammunition on the table next to her chair. Then he took a flashlight from his pocket. "New batteries. I'll be in the living room."

With Tony asleep in his crib, she curled up in the big rocking chair. And then she waited.

The loaded gun at her side didn't give her peace. Yes, they might need to protect themselves in a world that still wanted to annihilate their kind, but neither she nor David had ever wanted to have their gun-handling knowledge put to the test in a real life situation. And yet here they were.

She'd impressed the men at the range with her ability to get the job done and all her shots clustered in the black, with several in the bull's eye. Sometimes she even beat David's efforts, which brought raucous laughter from the guys who thought it cool that this little Israeli woman could shoot better than her strong, tall, ex-military husband, whose marksmanship made him formidable.

Other women didn't seem to frequent the range. Perhaps the men went home and told their wives about their neighbor the sharpshooter, the woman, the foreigner. No wonder they stared at her and never invited her over. She was too different. Which would make it easy for someone to find and target her. Them. Her baby.

Every dog's bark set her pulse soaring. A twig snapped outside her window, but would the sound of footsteps penetrate the glass panes?

No one looking in could see the rocker or the crib, but she had an angled view toward the yard. And so she watched.

When she felt her eyelids begin to close, she stood and walked to the crib. She touched her son's cheeks. They were still cool.

David must have heard her stirring. His whisper came from the doorway. "You okay? Need anything?"

"No, thanks."

Floorboards creaked even after she'd heard the sound of sagging springs in their old couch, long after there should have been only silence. She heard them and knew someone was sneaking in to get her, to hurt her baby, to destroy them all.

Was that plop-plop only water dripping in the basin?

That was *definitely* metal on metal. You couldn't miss metal on metal.

She grabbed the arms of the chair, and, instead of staring out at the night, she focused on the doorway. She should grab her gun, have it ready.

Tony fussed. *Oh, baby, don't,* she whispered soundlessly.

If someone walked the hall, he'd have gotten David first. He'd have to get past David, and no one would get past David, would they?

Maybe her husband had fallen asleep. Maybe it was all up to her now.

Please, Adonai, don't let David be hurt. Or worse.

She couldn't just sit here. What if her baby woke up? What if she were the only one between him and a madman?

She picked up her gun, checked the cylinder, and stood as carefully, as quietly as possible, before she tiptoed to the door. Listening, she eased out into the silent hall.

A soft snore came from the couch. She smiled. Not wounded, then.

Doing a walk-through of the house, checking out the windows, took a while. By the time she'd finished, she heard a snuffling from the nursery. She headed back to the sanctuary of her boy's room, set the gun within reach, and lifted Tony before his mumbles could turn into a full-fledged cry.

She changed him and gave him another dose of pain killer/fever reducer so he'd sleep at least another four hours. Whispering sweet nothings, she returned to the rocker with him nuzzled against her chest.

In spite of the fear that continued to hover, her body settled into the peace that filled her when she held her baby close. She'd do anything to keep him safe. Anything.

15 DAVID

1983

The bark or snort or whatever noise his throat made—or was that his nose?—startled him awake. For a moment, he couldn't remember why he was on the couch, his neck at a crick-inducing angle, instead of in his bed.

And then he glanced down. His gun rested near his thigh.

The dim light of dawn filtered through the uncurtained windows. He listened, waiting.

There it was, the soft creak of the rocker on the carpeted bedroom floor, whispered words from the back bedroom. He cleared his throat so he wouldn't startle Meira and headed in the direction of the nursery.

The sight that met him was one he'd never tire of. It made his heart catch, the beauty of his wife cradling their nursing son. David leaned against the doorjamb.

"Good morning," she whispered.

"Did you get any rest at all?"

She nodded. "I did. Not much, but enough."

"Good thing my vigilance wasn't needed."

Grinning, she said, "Good thing."

"Was I making a lot of noise?"

"No, not until that snort, which obviously woke you. I did a couple of walk-arounds when I thought I heard a bogeyman in the hall. It was just my imagination working overtime."

"I'll go fix coffee, then maybe take a check outside after I'm fortified."

"I could use a cup."

Tony raised his head to give his father a toothy grin.

"Those teeth look like they could do some damage. He's not biting you?"

Meira laughed. "He tried once. I discouraged him, and he hasn't since."

"Good thing."

They sipped their coffee while Tony played with his crib toys. And they tried to decide what to do next.

"You don't think he's found us, do you?" she asked.

"My guess is not yet. If he had, he'd have tried something last night."

"But just in case?"

"We'll check things out and make a few plans. We still don't know who, if anyone, followed Eli to the hotel."

"You think it could have involved something other than us—me—and that vendetta?"

"I hope so. Hope it has nothing to do with us."

"I'm hoping it was his overactive imagination."

David smiled over the rim of his cup. "You and me both."

"You want a bagel?" Meira asked.

"We have any eggs? I need protein."

She sliced a bagel and dropped it in the toaster. Then she got out eggs and a bowl, whipped up five, added seasonings, and sprinkled in some grated cheddar before folding the omelet. While it browned and the cheese melted, she slid the bagels on a plate, brought out cream cheese and strawberry jam, and refilled their cups.

"Smells wonderful," he told her when she handed over his share, the hefty, loaded-with-cheese portion of the omelet.

The doorbell rang as she was serving herself. "Da-vid." Her voice rippled with fear.

"Stay here." He picked up his gun, walked into the front hall, and called through the door. "Yes?"

No answer. He looked through the peephole. No one.

Unless the bell ringer was two feet tall.

"Anyone there?" he called again.

Silence answered.

Slowly, gun at the ready, he opened the door. There was no one, nothing. Not even a package.

He couldn't be sure the someone who'd hit the doorbell wasn't hiding around the corner or behind the car. The someone who might be trying to frighten them. Or more.

And then he heard giggling, followed by scuffling feet hitting the ground.

Kids. It had just been kids. Had they seen his gun? He hoped not. He could picture it now, them rushing home to tell their parents, make him out to be the neighborhood pariah.

He tucked his weapon in his waistband before returning to the kitchen. "I'd forgotten it's Saturday. Kids playing their games."

"That'll be Jay's boys from next door. Always trying to get attention."

"What they need is a little discipline." He lifted a forkful of cold omelet. "They may have seen my gun."

"I hope not. Jay's rabidly anti-everything."

"Including discipline."

Meira grinned. "Including."

"I'm not sure we ought to stay here, not as jumpy as we are—as I am." He sipped his coffee and topped it off with some from the pot to warm it up.

"Where do you plan on us going? You've still got to go to work on Monday."

"A motel. I'll make a few calls."

16   MEIRA

1983

The baby went down for a nap, and she began packing. Pulling things from drawers and fitting them into suitcases kept her hands busy, involving the automatic part of her brain. With the rest, she could cogitate about the something that had been bothering her during the night.

"David," she called quietly.

Toothbrush in hand, David poked his head out the bathroom door.

"I've been thinking."

He held up the brush. "Just a sec."

When he'd finished, he came in and sat next to the open suitcase. "Thinking about what?"

"How many people could actually be interested in me enough to come here? It's not like I'm actively working against them." She folded underwear and stuck it in between her shirts. "I can't see it. If the only motive is revenge, I can't imagine more than one person, that cousin, wanting it—unless the bomber had a huge family with a lot of money and nothing else to do. What would their motivation be to come all this way just for me when there's all of Israel to be attacked? Boredom?"

"Good question."

"Let's say the cousin and maybe a few others are furious that their brave fellow is dead. But he was killed years ago, so why now? And if my name were merely one of many on a list, why wouldn't they wait until I returned to Israel? How would they/he know my married name? How would he get into the States, much less come up with the resources to pay for a trip here?"

"I don't have an answer to that, but Eli seems to be worried about it enough to have warned us. He also thinks he was followed."

She stopped folding and stared at her husband. "David."

He must have heard something in the tone of her voice. He reached for her free hand. "Hmm?"

"What if Eli told us this only to frighten us so we'd go along with his plan?"

"You mean there may not be anyone after you? There may not have been a note with your name on it?"

It made sense. "I'm not worth the money or the time."

"Devil's advocate here. What if you represent something to this cousin and his cohorts? You got in their way. If they take you out, they make a statement. 'Look at us, we're mighty enough to finagle a visa and pluck the enemy right out of her safe little home in America.' You know Hezbollah and the

Iranians calls us the Great Satan and Israel the Little Satan."

"But these guys aren't Hezbollah." And she wasn't any kind of satan.

"We don't know how they see the U.S. We know they hate Israel, and America has stood on the side of Israel, which makes us their enemy. Eli said Fatah and PFLP have moved into Lebanon, making it a base for attacks over the border. I'd hate to imagine Eli, and by extension my uncle and your father, making up something just to get us involved in some scheme."

He was right. Of course, he was right. She sat down on his other side. "They wouldn't." She sighed. "But I'd much rather think about a wily Eli than about terrorists sneaking around Virginia trying to grab us."

"They may not be. You could be absolutely right, especially when you suggest that the resources needed to come after you would be substantial."

She smiled at him. "You think so?"

"I do. But, just in case we're wrong, we need to go to a motel and wait this out. It shouldn't take long once Eli's people get involved. I'll give him a call."

Maybe Eli would come through right away and maybe he wouldn't. She dreaded the idea of spending her days in a cramped room with a baby while David went to work. "You'd better find a place near a restaurant. I don't want to be stuck alone without a kitchen or a way to feed us."

He looked surprised by that thought. "What a fool I am. I never considered what this would be like for you with a baby. Forget my job. I won't be going to work until we can move back into our house safely."

If they'd ever be able to.

17 Meira

She was running out of emotional space as they told their story. It was time to cull out the junk crammed into her brain and get down to the bits worth keeping. But how was she supposed to determine which those were?

There was no how-to manual for spies who came out of the cold and spilled all to their son. No automatic pass that says tell the story and everyone will be happy in the end. She felt wrung out. Stretched to breaking. Tony's sulks as they talked about the episode in Virginia had just about worn her out. Instead of sending him to bed for a three-day nap, she'd like to crawl into her own and have David come get her when it was all over.

Coward.

Yes. She'd raise her hand and admit it.

Tony drew his right foot to his knee and retied his well-tied laces before repeating the process with his left. Next, he wiggled back into a couch pillow, never looking up at them.

"You okay?" His father asked. She wished he'd ask her.

Tony's shrug, which used his shoulders and his face, stole even more of her emotional space. "Why do you guys keep quitting the story?" he asked.

"It's hard to tell all at once," she admitted. "It was a very emotional time."

"Yeah, but it was so long ago. And you lived, so what's the big deal?"

Teenage indifference coupled with anger? Where was her sign-out-of-school sheet?

"Fine," she said and began talking.

ⵊ

1983

Main Street boasted a post office, a hardware store, a small grocery, two B&Bs, and a fish market with a pier where all the local fishermen unloaded their catch. Behind Main Street were smaller roads where most of the locals lived and one that meandered out of town along the river.

David and Meira's house was about a mile out of town along the river road, not prime real estate, but quaint. Their nearest neighbor, Jay, lived with his wife, Cherry, and four boys in a house that had been added onto through the years by people who forgot to consult an architect. A hedge, through which Jay's children liked to wiggle on a regular basis, separated the driveways and back yards. Meira found it interesting that those children were never referred to as his wife's, as if Cherry didn't have anything to do with raising or disciplining them. Which may have been the absolute truth.

FROM FIRE INTO FIRE

On the other side of their property, a row of weeping willows gave a visual separation to a lot with only the charred foundation of a house and a barn crammed with various fishing boats.

Meira checked the rooms to see if she'd forgotten anything. While David loaded their car, she collected supplies for the baby, along with some food she could keep in a motel room.

"Jay must have taken the boys somewhere," David said as he picked up Tony and his diaper bag, "or set them in front of the television. Either way, I'm grateful I didn't see anyone. If no one knows we've gone, no one can talk."

He settled them in the backseat, climbed behind the wheel, and started the car. As he backed out of the driveway and headed toward the village, he said, "I'm going to stop at the market to pick up some ice for the cooler."

Meira waited with Tony on her lap in the back seat. He was fascinated by the sights outside the window and pressed his nose up close to watch the comings and goings while his daddy went in search of ice.

Exhausted, she closed her eyes, only opening them when Tony patted her cheeks to draw her attention back to him. She laughed and kissed the tip of his nose. That seemed to satisfy him, because he turned again to look out. She followed his gaze.

And saw Abreeq, the bomber's cousin, whose name meant *glittering sword*. He seemed to be asking directions from, of all people, Cherry. Her next-door neighbor. Cherry pointed down the road and waved, as if to indicate that the road continued on out of town. On toward Cherry's house. On toward Meira's.

Cherry didn't look toward the street or at their car or seem to pay attention to anything that wasn't right in front of her. Like the attractive Arab.

Who'd come all this way, all this very long way, to take out her and hers.

Meira titled sideways so her head wasn't visible through the window. Abreeq wouldn't recognize her baby, and she'd be surprised if Cherry knew what Tony looked like.

But Abreeq would recognize David. Meira willed her husband to stay in the store a little longer and even whispered a prayer that he and they would remain hidden.

When David opened the car door next to the cooler to fill it with ice, she sat up and stuttered, "He's here." She glanced around. Both Abreeq and Cherry were gone.

"What?" David asked.

"Abreeq. I saw him."

David dropped the ice into the cooler and climbed in the front. "Where?" he asked as he turned the ignition key.

"He was talking to Jay's wife. I imagine he's on his way to our house now."

"Where can I leave you and Tony?"

"David, no. Call Eli. Call the police. You can't go there. We'll just leave."

He turned around in his seat. "If we leave, there's no guarantee he'll be caught and locked up. Say a deputy goes to the house, confronts him, and he runs. Or he shoots the deputy, who probably won't be expecting a mad Arab with nothing to lose, even if we could warn the sheriff. It's not like they have any experience with crazies of this magnitude in rural Virginia. And if Abreeq gets away, we'll have to keep running and looking over our shoulders for the rest of our lives. I can't let that happen."

"Then drive us to Miss Emma's house. If she's home, she'll take Tony. I'll go with you. Two guns are better than one. And you know I shoot as well as you do."

"And probably better than the locals."

Miss Emma lived on a back street in a small clapboard house, supplementing her Social Security payments by helping out where she could, including babysitting and housecleaning. Meira liked and trusted her.

When they pulled up to her house and saw her car in the driveway, Meira realized just how tightly she'd been clenching her teeth. Without Miss Emma, she'd have no one she could call on. "She's here."

"Come on. We'll ask to use her phone, too."

The older lady seemed happy to see them. "You leave that sweet lamb right here with me. The phone's in there, Mr. David," she said, pointing to the kitchen.

When they were ready to leave, David said, "We'll be back as soon as we can." He handed her a scribbled note with Eli's name. "Here's an emergency contact."

"Tony's teething," Meira said, "but I think he'll be okay."

"If he gets fussy, I know what to do," Miss Emma said. "Don't you worry."

Meira hugged her baby as close to her as she could without scaring him. "Be a good boy for Miss Emma. We'll see you soon."

Adonai, please, make it so. Help us. Protect us.

Back in the car, David took her hand. "Eli told me just to keep an eye on the man and his car, but on no account to play the hero. He's calling for help."

"Is that what we're going to do?"

"If possible, yes." He opened the glove compartment and

removed his weapon. "Yours?"

"In my bag in the back."

"Get it now. We need to be ready."

A car she didn't recognize sat in front of the boat barn on their neighbor's property. David drove slowly past their house.

"No one," she said. "Do you think he got inside?"

"Probably. I'm going to park. We'll head back on foot."

"Do you think that's wise? He's probably armed, too."

"If we go in the back way and hide behind the boat barn, we should have a decent view of our place." He turned around and headed back in the direction of town. "You get down out of sight. I'm going to pull off in that picnic area in the woods."

"I guess anywhere else would be too conspicuous." She scooted low in the seat and folded herself toward David. "Good thing I'm tiny enough to do this."

He rested one hand on her head. "Tiny is perfect."

Tires crunched on gravel, and she knew they'd turned into the picnic area. She sat up. There were only two tables, a portable toilet, and a water fountain, but it was shaded by trees on three sides. A nice breeze usually blew off the water, making it a popular place for picnickers who didn't have their own waterfront property.

"I need to put on another shirt to hide my gun," she said.

David opened the trunk, moved Tony's case to get to hers, and opened it for her. She dug around until she found a long-sleeved work shirt.

"What about you?" she asked.

"I'm fine, but get a hat. Mine's in the back seat."

"I'm not sure I packed one."

"You always have a hat of some sort."

"I was in a hurry."

He unloaded bags until he could get to his toolbox from which he pulled out his oldest ball cap. He put it on and then retrieved the broad-brimmed crushable hat she'd bought him for fishing. It dwarfed her head, but at least she'd be harder to recognize.

David led them along the edge of the woods until they came to a curve in the road and the open field of their neighbor's half-acre. There was no sign of any activity as they sauntered across it, camouflaged, they hoped, by their hats and the unexpectedness of their route.

The car was still parked in front of the barn. "Quiet now," David said as he crept toward the row of weeping willows.

They crouched low under the ground-sweeping branches and waited, listening. They couldn't see into the house. The only windows at the end of the house were the high bathroom window and one in their bedroom.

"I wonder if Eli managed to get through to anyone." Meira kept her voice just above a whisper.

Would the sheriff or FBI believe him? How long would it take the communications to go from him to Israel and back?

A back door slammed in the distance and boys' voices called to each other. She prayed they'd stay in their own yard. A ball thumped on the neighbor's driveway and then slammed against their garage. Maybe basketball would keep them occupied, and they wouldn't try to play any more pranks. She didn't want them anywhere near Abreeq.

"I'm going to try to get behind the shed," David said. "I need a better view of the back yard."

"I'll cover you," she said. "Just be careful."

He leaned in and gave her a quick kiss. "Keep alert. If he

comes out the front and heads toward his car, you'll be exposed here."

18 DAVID

1983

He'd never thought of himself as a warrior, mostly because he'd never had to be, not even in the Navy. Yes, he'd been trained, but that had been all. And although he'd been called on to protect Meira back in the day, he'd never had to wield a loaded gun in the direction of real people. Real villains.

Good thing they'd practiced shooting at paper people and cardboard targets. Maybe his steady hand from the practice range wouldn't translate to a perfectly steady aim when he confronted a breathing human, but all that practice had been for just-in-case. And their just-in-case had come. They were in a battle against a murderous terrorist gunning for David's family.

He kept low as he crossed the yard. Low and, he hoped,

invisible. The closer he got to the shed, the louder those kids' voices sounded.

Boredom got kids like that into mischief, and they loved using his house as one of their mischief-making playgrounds along with another neighbor's trailered runabout, which they'd festooned with toilet paper streamers one night. The owner had been livid, his language not something those boys should have had to hear.

And yet, hadn't David wanted to see their hides tanned a few times? Meira said they needed their parents' attention. Maybe. And maybe they needed a good spanking along with lessons in manners and a few rules.

David bent low at the side of the shed and then eased to its corner, scanning the back porch and as much of the driveway and hedge as he could see. He checked his gun and watched the house. Surely, if someone were in there, David would eventually see movement.

He thought of his namesake, the David of the Psalms, who'd written in the twenty-seventh psalm, "Adonai is my light and my salvation—whom do I need to fear? Adonai is the stronghold of my life—of whom shall I be afraid?"

He'd try to hang on to that, the words of an imperfect king who had gone against giants when he was just a boy. Perhaps he, a present-day and just-as-imperfect David, could go against this enemy and win.

A shadow crossed the dining-room window and moved away. David waited a beat, then dashed to the house, ducked under that same window, and pressed up against the wall, his gun at the ready as he peeked inside.

19 Meira

1983

Meira eased some of the willow's fronds out of her way. There was something . . . something that didn't belong, a silhouette hiding in their hedge.

David had dashed out of sight, supposedly toward the house, exposing himself, which he'd only have done if he knew where Abreeq was at that moment. Had one of those kids pushed into the hedge, into that space between two bushes she'd hoped would fill in with new growth? It was the perfect size to hide in, and they'd used it before. She'd seen them dodging through her backyard in a game of hide and seek.

The boys called to one another. The ball thumped on the concrete driveway or the backboard. Occasionally a shot went astray, and someone scurried after it. So, why was one of them—and it had to be one of the older ones—hiding here?

She squinted at the shape.

One of the older ones? The oldest was only twelve. He was small. Whoever had just moved inside the hedge looked more like a teenager.

She couldn't let a child be caught in the crossfire, or have David's life be put at risk by a prankster.

She checked her gun. *Lord, please let me not have to use it.* She didn't want to have to kill anyone. Still, she set her feet, ready to bolt if David needed her.

And several things happened at once.

The basketball shot over the hedge into their yard. The figure stepped out from its hiding place in the bushes. And the boys shouted that somebody had to get the ball.

The figure was a woman, a woman who now raised her arm as if to take aim at David. Meira screamed. The woman pivoted, jerking her gun in Meira's direction.

And two shots rang out. She had no idea who, other than the woman, had pulled a trigger. She prayed the other was David.

She was already dashing toward the house, heedless of danger, her gun ready. Her feet slapped dry grass.

O Lord, don't let David be hurt. Please, I beg of You.

Chaos had escalated by the time she made it to the corner of the house. David lay sprawled on top of the woman. All four boys had climbed through the hedge and were closing in on the figures lying there, surrounding them, just as Abreeq pushed open the screen door and walked out onto the stoop.

Meira backed out of sight as Abreeq waved his gun in the air and shouted in Arabic for the boys to go, get out of there, go home. They just stared at him, open-mouthed.

It would have been amusing if fear hadn't taken hold of her. Her first thought was to distract Abreeq by getting him to chase her, but those foolish boys might just come, too.

The length of the house stood between her and them. She'd accomplish nothing by running toward the chaos, and she couldn't risk trying to shoot Abreeq from here. If she missed—and the likelihood of that was too great for her to want to chance it because to take aim properly, she'd have to step away from the house, which would give him time to aim at her—she'd become another target for a man who probably had twice the training she did. Maybe ten times her training because he was bound to have killed before.

Wisdom, please, Adonai. And reinforcements—soon? She sprinted for the front door. She didn't have her keys, so she could only hope the spare was still hidden under the ceramic frog at the base of her favorite azalea.

It was. Hurrying up the front steps, she slid the key in the lock and opened the door, grateful that David kept the hinges oiled. As she slid off her shoes, the image of David's baseball bat surfaced. She tiptoed to the hall closet, grabbed the bat, and moved stealthily toward the back of the house.

The door to the yard opened off the kitchen. Tucking her gun in easy reach in her waistband—because she really hoped she wouldn't have to kill the man—she checked out the dining-room hutch and the archway into the kitchen. A plan had formed. She leaned the bat against the wall, grabbed the large Rose Medallion bowl that decorated the table, and—sparing barely a moment to regret the lovely reproduction piece—shot up another prayer and heaved the bowl against the far wall. It shattered. She hefted the bat and flattened herself out of sight behind the hutch.

The screen door opened and slammed shut, feet hit the linoleum. Meira held her breath as he waited a few heartbeats before creeping forward.

Her pulse sped. She breathed as she'd been taught, carefully in and out, imagining each breath sounded like a roaring hiss, because that's what she thought she heard.

On he came. Long minutes passed. She imagined him wondering who lay in wait and if that person had a gun.

Was Abreeq at the threshold yet? Ah, a board creaked. He'd hit the hardwood. One more step, please don't let him look this way.

She raised the bat, stepped out, and swung. The bat connected with his outstretched arm and continued to his gut. His gun bounced to the floor, and Abreeq cried out as he bent, stumbling forward and giving Meira time to raise the bat again and bring it down hard on the back of his head. He fell in a heap.

Tires screeched out front, one car and then another, but Meira could only think of David. She ran to the splintered back door. All four boys—what *were* their names?—had started babbling again and pushing each other. David, her beloved, looked up from where he now straddled an angry and bleeding woman who seemed to be pressing what looked like half of David's shirt against her shoulder.

"You got him?" David asked her, a smile playing on his lips.

She started the few yards toward him, but tears welled, and she collapsed to the stoop. "I thought he'd shot you."

"I'm fine, love. I'm grateful you are, too."

All the children began talking at once when Sheriff Jones

and a deputy strode up the driveway. Another deputy, his gun at the ready, came around the other side of the house.

She'd met the sheriff once, at a bake sale for the local school band. She pushed herself to her feet.

He nodded at her. "Mrs. Rassadim." To David, he said, "And Mr. Rassadim? We got a call that you might need help. Who do you have there?"

David stood, gathering the extra gun and the bullets and handing them to the sheriff. "I'm not sure who she is. She tried to shoot my wife. I shot to stop her. Obviously, my aim failed."

"His tackle was super," the oldest boy said. "I was the first one through." He pointed to the hole between the bushes. "We came to get our ball."

"And then the bad guy came out of the house," said one of the middle boys.

"He talked funny." That was the youngest one. "We didn't understand him."

David draped an arm around her shoulder, and she leaned into him. Speaking to the sheriff, she gave him Abreeq's name and said, "He tried to get the boys to leave or at least to get out of his way, probably so he could shoot David, but I'm not sure he even realized he was yelling at them in Arabic. He's inside. I hit him with a baseball bat."

The sheriff motioned one of the deputies toward the door, but before he could say anything, the woman on the ground kicked a booted foot, obviously in frustration, and called to Meira. "You. You will die. One day, you who killed my brother, will die. That is my promise. *Allahu Akbar!*" Then she switched to Arabic and peppered the air with curses.

"That's enough out of you," Sheriff Jones said. "John-Jay,

cuff her and then call for an ambulance."

Over the curses that spewed from the woman as a deputy restrained her, Meira said, "I only knocked him out. I didn't kill him."

"*Bah.* Not Abreeq. My brother Salim. He is dead because of you."

"You mean the bomber in Jerusalem? His name was Salim?"

"My brother. He was a brave fighter for our people."

"Not true. He murdered many, and he died trying to kill again."

One of the boys ran toward the front to check out a dark gray car that pulled into the driveway. The new arrivals looked like standard-issue movie detectives, decked out in suits and sunglasses.

They flashed their badges at the sheriff. "Agent Howland and Agent Reynolds."

While the FBI and the locals talked, David drew Meira close. She whispered into his shoulder. "I was so afraid." Her voice shook. "For all of you."

"Yeah, well, I had a few bad moments myself." He released her.

The agents headed into the house, and Sheriff Jones crouched in front of the boys. "Is your dad around, Tommy?" he asked the oldest.

Interesting, Meira thought, that the sheriff hadn't asked about Cherry.

"Nah. He had to go into town to get Mom and do some shopping. She was gonna have her hair fixed."

"I'm thinking," Meira said, addressing the crowd, "that when things calm down around here—maybe tomorrow afternoon—we need to have an ice cream party. In honor of such brave boys."

Four pairs of eyes lit. "Can we have chocolate with sprinkles?" the little one asked.

"Absolutely," Meira said. "Chocolate is my favorite."

"With sprinkles."

"Definitely with sprinkles."

The sheriff stood. "I think it's time you boys got your ball and headed on home. I'll stop by to see your dad later, hear?"

"Yes, sir," the one named Tommy said. "We're not in trouble, are we?"

"Not at all." He ruffled Tommy's hair.

Meira felt tears well as she looked at the young faces. Maybe what happened today would get their parents' attention focused back where it ought to be on their precious boys.

And then the sheriff turned to David. "Mr. Rassadim, I've got to ask if you have a permit for that gun of yours."

20 Meira

Meira paused in her story telling and looked from David to Tony. "I'm tired," she said. "I think I'd like to quit for an hour or so and take a walk. Would that be okay?"

"Absolutely," David said. "It's a gorgeous afternoon, and we could all use a time out." He turned to Tony. "What about you?"

"I'm not tired."

"Then why don't you go for a walk with your mother. I've got some phone calls to make."

"Nah," Tony said. "Can I use your computer?"

David checked with her. At her shrug, he said, "Sure. For an hour, but that's all." But he was speaking to Tony's back as the boy headed to the small den. "You're welcome!" he called.

Tony turned and shouted a rueful, "Thanks!"

"He probably feels as if he's been let out of jail," Meira said.

"You okay?" David asked as she dug around in the coat closet for the walking shoes she kept for lakeside use.

"Exhausted. Who knew telling a story could be such hard work." She checked her shoes for bugs and then pulled them on over her socks. "A walk will do me good."

He bent to kiss her forehead. "See you soon."

A breeze seemed to be coming from the north, a change from the normal westerlies that might indicate a storm brewing up in Canada, perhaps bringing some much-needed rain. She sniffed clean air with none of the odors she'd grown so used to in the streets of Beirut, where spice scents mingled with sweat and dirt and sometimes even with sewage. There, a wind shift off the sea cleansed the air, brought other smells, more welcome ones.

Here, too, it was quieter. She reveled in the difference: bird chatter as opposed to human cries. Engines revving around the lake were few, and raised voices even fewer.

Her muscles had needed this. The tension of these days had taken a toll on more than just her stomach. She increased her pace as she headed right onto the narrow road that circled the lake. It was only used by residents at this end, residents and their guests and the occasional delivery. Almost everyone received their mail at the small post office in town; it was safer that way for those who didn't live here full time.

She met only one car. The driver waved but didn't stop. Most of the homes were set back closer to the lake than the road, so she had the patched macadam to herself and the slap-slap of her soles as she finished a mile, then two, before turning back.

Remembering Virginia, her fear for her baby and her husband, had been hard on her. Telling the whole, reliving it, had taken a toll. Maybe now she could continue, finish the tale, and await her son's judgement. Maybe now she'd be strong enough to help him through the process—at least for today.

And later, when it was over, perhaps she'd be able to open her paints? Pick up her pencils? Actually create here in this gorgeous place?

David suggested they gather on the porch to enjoy the breeze. "And the view's better."

When they were settled, each in one of the Adirondack chairs at the other end of the porch from the swing, he picked up where they'd left off. "The two who'd come after your mother, Abreeq and Salim's sister—I don't remember her name, do you?" he turned to ask her.

She shook her head. She wasn't sure she'd ever heard it.

"Anyway, although they were headed to prison," David said, "we couldn't be sure they were the only ones who'd come, so we still had to do something."

Tony shook his head. "I don't get it. You keep talking about those words they said, all of them, when they tried to kill you."

"What words?"

"*Allahu Akbar,* Allah is great. I mean, I've heard people saying it all my life, and nobody was murdering anyone else."

"They're proclaiming a lot more than 'Allah is great'," David said. "They're actually stating that he is *greater* than any other god. They're deceived, and they've been taught that all who refuse to follow Islam must be killed. Especially all Jews."

They were also words that would haunt Meira forever.

Each time she heard them, she imagined the knife blade slashing toward her or the gun's black hole aimed at her, at David. And yet her son needed to see her as rational woman who based her choices on what was right, not on fears she'd accumulated since that day in 1979.

She took a deep, cleansing breath and said, "Many followers of Islam, especially among the Shia, consider *jihad*—holy war—an imperative of their religion, a call to destroy all who won't follow their faith. And it's not just the Shia who believe the Koran calls them to avenge the death of family members."

"But you didn't kill anyone." Tony's voice and his face showed the worry he carried, a worry they'd handed him on a platter. A silver one.

This parenting business was heartbreaking.

"No, I didn't," she said. "But angry people aren't always reasonable. And those who have been taught hatred from an early age lose the power to discern right from wrong. That's why so many who fled Israel in the late forties have joined groups like Al Fatah and the Popular Front."

"Weren't they forced to leave their homes? That's what Bahir's tutor said. That the Jews knocked on their doors with guns and promised they'd shoot everyone who didn't go away. Then the Jews took their houses."

"That's not what happened," Meira said. "It is what some of the Palestinians—the ones who left—told themselves and their children when they found themselves in camps. Camps they're still in. Most fled because their leaders, including the Mufti of Jerusalem, told them to go. There was a huge power struggle for control of the land by Arab leaders, especially between the then King of Jordan, Abdullah I, and the Mufti."

"The camps are horrible places. I've seen pictures," Tony said.

"They are. And no one in power in Jordan, Syria, or Lebanon tried to resettle the refugees. Instead, they used them for their own political gain."

"Or what they thought would be their gain," David said.

Tony leaned forward in his chair and glanced quickly from one parent to the other. "Bahir's tutor said we should make war against Israel so the people could leave the camps and go home."

"Bloodshed is never the answer," David said. "We can't let it be the answer."

"That's why you do what you do?"

"That's it," his father said. "That and to keep you and your mom safe."

"But I still don't get why you had to lie to me. And why we couldn't just be normal people."

"Because normal was stolen from us the moment I witnessed the bombing," Meira said. "Because a crazy man's family wanted revenge for something I didn't cause."

"And we couldn't be sure it would ever end. Two more were in jail, but what about others? And what about their neighbors and friends, others who'd sworn vengeance on Jews? We were Jews."

"I've gotta go pee," Tony said, standing. "But I want to know what happened next."

1983

Eli had shown up soon after the FBI agents. Meira left them to talk—and David to sweep up the broken vase—while she went to pick up the baby.

When they finally got rid of law enforcement, Meira ordered pizza and David and Eli unloaded the car. They purposefully didn't discuss the afternoon's events until she'd fed Tony and put him down for the night. Poor baby needed another dose of painkiller to help him settle.

"I never want to go through that again," Meira said, taking a seat next to David and drawing his hand into her lap. "Whatever it takes. And I want my baby protected."

"Whatever it takes." David squeezed her hand.

Eli, in the obnoxiously optimistic manner of someone who'd been certain of getting his way, opened his briefcase and passed over the paperwork, the plan of action, and two new passports. And where, David wanted to know, had he gotten the photographs for those?

Eli just laughed, ignoring the question. "As far as your employers here are concerned, you'll be leaving for family reasons." He also ignored David's scowl. "You have your masters in engineering. You need your PhD. MIT is willing to take you."

"And where did this fictional me get his masters?"

"Cal Poly."

David turned to Meira. "California Polytechnic University." And then he asked Eli, "You said the nickname as if you'd been there."

"I've done my homework, cousin. We tried to find a school where no one would know you as David Rassadim, the Jew, or wonder why they hadn't met you as Da'oud Rassad, the Arab. Cal Poly has many foreign students, which means this new you could have easily been lost in the throng."

"Great. It's a good thing I actually have a degree, but as it wasn't from MIT, I'm wondering how hard their PhD program will be."

"You'll have a tutor if you need one."

"So, one tutor for Arabic and one for engineering. I rate."

"First the Arabic. You can't come out as an Arab-American until you have some familiarity with that language. You'll need to hide out somewhere while you study."

David glanced over at Meira. "I recently inherited a lake cottage from an elderly cousin, and the deed is still in her name. I don't know if you can do anything about transferring it to this new persona."

"I take it the cottage is relatively remote? Do the neighbors know you?"

"It wasn't a place for socializing with anyone but family. We visited in the summer, but I'm sure no one in the neighborhood would remember me. After the aunt died, my parents used the place for summer vacations, but they lived in Florida."

"Then we should be able to make that work."

Meira sighed. "I can't get over the fact that this whole idea for using civilians came from a task force my father helped set up."

"You should call your parents." Eli glanced at his watch. "Maybe first thing in the morning."

"Will my father already know about Abreeq and what's-her-name?"

"I don't know," he said. "It's possible. He knew about the threat to you. He may have asked to be let in on whatever happened. After all, you're his."

"It's hard to believe he's behind this, that he thinks our entering this program is a good idea. I mean, maybe in the abstract, for someone else, but for *me*, his own daughter? For

David and Tony?"

Eli had the grace to look apologetic. "I'm sure he imagines we can do a better job of protecting you in this kind of mission than we can with you running around under your own name. And certainly better than you can do trying to hide on your own."

The years had changed them all, hadn't they? The years and her choices. Not to mention, the choices of madmen.

Sleep eventually overtook David, but Meira's mind wouldn't hush. It whispered hard words and conjured images of murder, mayhem, and raging hordes of angry people. She continued to see Abreeq holding a gun, David lying on top of the woman, Abreeq crumbled and his head bashed. The children standing there, staring at the crazy man with the gun.

She'd run from one madman. For the sake of her family, she'd fled Israel and made a home here, and the result had been more than she could have imagined back when she'd said that hasty "I do."

Now that her comfortable lifestyle was threatened and chaos had knocked at the door in the guise of Palestinian terrorists and Eli's henchmen, all she wanted was to hold that life close. Running from trouble wasn't in her nature, or in David's. And yet to protect their baby, they'd have to run again, in case more of the bomber's cousins or sisters showed up armed and ready.

The plan Eli had set before them seemed horribly convoluted. And frightening. Were they smart enough to juggle a new identity? And could the powers that be really guarantee the safety of their son? What exactly would they tell him? And when?

Or should they just take Tony and run, figure this mess out and hide on their own. Her thoughts ping-ponged. Do it, don't do it.

Of course, if Eli's plans gelled, they could work from within the United States until things settled down in Lebanon. And if that were possible, could she—they—turn this down? It felt as if they'd be repudiating the homeland's request for help if they said no.

Their people had such a rich and varied history in the land. Many had stood on the front lines, believing in the cause and in HaShem's eternal promises, trusting that the Almighty would go before them into battle. Aba used to read the Scriptures aloud every Sabbath and many evenings as well. Now, Meira lay in her comfortable bed, listening to her husband's soft breathing, and thought of the story of Joshua fighting the Amalekites in the valley while Moses, Aaron, and Hur went up the mountain. As long as Moses kept his hands raised in praise, the army of Israel won; when he let them fall in exhaustion, the army lost ground. She always felt a shiver run through her when Aba read of the two men with Moses who stepped forward to help, propping up his arms when he tired.

Friends, brothers, family helped. Helping each other was what the people of HaShem had been taught to do. So were she and David supposed to act as an Aaron and a Hur to help their beloved Israel hold up her hands and win the battle?

She knew better than to ask for guarantees. They didn't exist. Violence happened. Crazy people carried guns. Cars sped out of control. Life was risky and would remain risky, even if they holed up at the lake cottage for the rest of their lives.

She tossed and turned for hours, begging for peace and

clarity. And she remembered her father's words whispered throughout her childhood. "If you don't know which way to choose, just wait. Wisdom comes in the waiting."

21 DAVID

The early afternoon breeze made David itch to get out on the water. He hadn't taken the Laser out since last summer, and now Meira was grocery shopping, and the kid was sitting on the front porch, staring out at the lake and brooding. It was time for some male bonding on a boat.

He pushed open the screen door. "You up for a sail?"

No answer. David gave it a moment and was finally rewarded with a shrug and a nod.

"I'll fill a thermos, grab a snack," he said. "You put on your swim trunks. Oh, and get sunscreen."

They dragged the small Laser down to the water's edge, rigged it, and pushed off, David at the helm until they were far enough out for the wind not to be worrying itself around trees and headlands. He eyed Tony. "Why don't you take the tiller?"

"Me?"

"Have you forgotten all I showed you last summer?"

"Hope not."

"Well, come on then. We'll have another lesson."

The wind was steady, if light, and pushed the small boat along at an easy pace. When they needed to tack, Tony called out the appropriate words but then pulled the tiller the wrong way, into a jibe.

David caught the boom before it slammed across the boat. Tony stared at it. "What'd I do wrong?"

"Let's go back over the how-tos of tacking, shall we? What is coming about and what is a jibe? Why do we want to control what happens?"

"So we don't tip and capsize."

"That's right. Nothing wrong with a good, controlled jibe, but if it happens by accident, especially in a wind, it can do some damage."

Tony listened and practiced and soon had the technique and the nomenclature learned. "Thanks, Dad," he said as they tacked toward home.

"They have sailing at this school you'll be attending."

"They do?"

"And rowing and all sorts of other sports."

"I'm sorry I got so mad at you guys. But I still wish you hadn't lied to me."

"I know. I wish we hadn't felt we had to."

"I mean, I get why you figured you had to protect Mom and me. They were kind of nasty people."

"Very. But do you also get why we work in Lebanon?"

"I guess so. Because of world peace." Tony grabbed the sheet and pulled it in when the sail started to luff.

"Well, that's a rather grandiose way to describe our meager contribution in the battle against madmen," David said as Tony played the line until he had the sail where it needed to be. "Good job on sail trim. Soon, you should be able to take the boat out by yourself. What do you think of that?"

Tony grinned, his eyes brightening. "And get really good before I go to the school? Maybe they race. Maybe I could get good enough to win."

"No reason why not. You have your own boat right here."

"That'd be cool. And maybe before I go, I'll grow some. I don't wanna be the only freshman who looks like a kid."

David laughed. "You won't be. It's happening."

"It is?"

"Absolutely. I can tell."

They tacked around the floating platform in the middle of the lake. "I want to swim out to here this summer. You think I can?"

David gauged the distance between their dock and the platform. "We can certainly build up to it. Maybe do it together, a little farther every day. That work for you?"

"I wanted to send Bahir a picture when I made it. Can I still do that?"

"Sure you can. No one said you have to quit writing to him. You'll just have to figure out how to keep your letters to things you're doing here or at your new school."

"Nothing about being a Jew."

"Right."

Tony pointed the Laser's bow straight for the bank, signaling David to raise the centerboard.

"Good landing," David said when the hull crunched on the sand.

After they lowered the sail and tied it to the boom, Tony said, "I'm going to miss Bahir."

"I know you will. And maybe one day you'll see him again." Although David didn't know how that could be managed until Tony had fully embraced his heritage. And then how would it work? Tony wouldn't want to lie.

Which must have been worrying him, because he said, "But I I'll never be able to tell him the truth about us. He'd never understand."

"No, and it would put us and our mission in danger."

Tony ducked his head. "I'm not sure how to be a Jew." Glancing up, he said, "Can I tell you something?"

"Anything."

"Knowing I'm one still kinda makes my stomach hurt."

"I'm sure it does." And Tony's admission brought a stabbing pain to the area of David's heart. "It's a leap."

"I mean, I know you guys never said bad things about Jews, because you wouldn't, would you? You being Jews and all. But some of my friends? They hate Jews."

David waited.

"So, if they knew about me, they'd hate me."

They'd reached the front porch. "Sit with me." David lowered himself to the bottom step and stretched his long legs out on the flagstone walk. He shot up a prayer for wisdom. "Let's consider that for a moment."

When he braced his elbows on his knees, Tony did the same. David didn't smile, although the mimicry pleased him—and made him hope wisdom would shine through his words.

"Are you any different today than you were last week? I mean, other than knowing something new. You're the same boy, aren't you?"

Tony nodded, frowning.

"Why would they hate you when they liked you last week?"

"They hate all Jews."

"Ah, so the prejudice isn't because of something real, then?"

"They think it's real."

"Yes, but is it? Are you a different person because you were born into a Jewish family instead of a Muslim or Christian one? Does your heritage change your inherent worth as an individual?"

"I guess not." Tony thought for a minute. "So, you're saying they're wrong about Jews."

"Any time someone hates an entire group of people because of who they are, that's wrong."

"But they hate Israelis because of what they've done. Because they stole the land."

"They didn't, but again, that's a debate for later. I'll give you some history books, stories of the region. And remember, a large number of Arabs remained in the land and are Israeli citizens. I read recently one Muslim reporter saying he'd rather be a second-class citizen in Israel than a first-class citizen in Cairo, Amman, or Damascus. Do you realize there are Muslims in the Israeli military? In the Israeli parliament?"

"Really? I thought the Jews just wanted Israel for Jews."

David wasn't going there. As far as he was concerned, it would have been easier if they had. Not as fair, perhaps, not as tolerant, but a whole lot easier. "It's important for us all to see people as individuals," he said, taking the high moral ground. "Some are misguided, and some use that as an excuse for murder and war. The Islamic extremists are the ones your mother and I and our family in Israel are trying to stop."

"Like the people who tried to kill Mom."

"Like them. Mom was an innocent, but to them, she had become the enemy. And many of those who call themselves freedom fighters are targeting other innocents like her with their car bombs and their guns."

"It's wrong."

"Very wrong."

"Can I tell you something else?" Tony asked. "I'm still kinda mad about it all."

"I know that, too."

Tony looked sideways at him. "You're not mad at me?"

"No. I get it. I'd be angry, too, if I were kept in the dark about something as big as this."

"Okay." Another pause. "You think there'll ever be peace? You know, where Bahir and his family can be okay with me not being the same as them?"

Peace? Not in a world where too many considered *jihad* a legitimate means of conversion and taught adherents to fear and hate those who didn't bow to their particular god. But among individuals? He was certain Nasri and his wife would accept them as Jews—if he were free to break his silence and speak truth. He told Tony as much.

"Does that mean lies are sometimes okay?" Tony asked. "I mean, do you think your lies don't count?"

There it was, the Question. David dragged his fingers through his hair and let out a long sigh. "Your mom and I have debated this many times. We know God hates liars. But He also instructed his servants to be cunning against the enemy."

"Bahir isn't an enemy."

"No, he's not. And yet he and his family are surrounded by

those who are. Those who want all of us dead just because we're Jews. And if we want to stop the men whose goal is to destroy our nation and our people, we must be cunning enough to uncover their plots. As we told you before, we've only lied overtly in our name change. For the rest, we've merely omitted the truth. And that's not difficult among the university crowd. Engineering doesn't lend itself to heavy discussions about faith, which means no one thinks about our silence on the matter of Islam. Because we speak Arabic, live in Lebanon, and observe Muslim prohibitions and holidays, others make assumptions about our belief system. Does that make sense? Do you understand what I'm trying to say?"

"Like Bahir's uncle says he doesn't believe in Allah, but he fits in?"

"That's much the same, except that Bahir's uncle wants to convert everyone to his unbelief." David laughed.

Tony's eyes danced. "He does! He really likes to argue, doesn't he?"

"I've had to bite my tongue at least once during every conversation with the man. But he has a good heart."

"Bahir's dad wants peace. He said so." Tony's young voice sounded wistful.

"I know," David said, wishing he could offer hope that it would be so. "He's a good man."

"But you don't tell him the truth."

Deep waters again. "I'm sorry I can't."

"Is it because you don't want him to have to lie to other people? You know, to cover up your secret?"

David had asked for wisdom, and his son had provided the nugget of truth they could hold to. "That's it exactly."

A slouch curved Tony's back as he reached between his

knees to pick up a small rock. David waited as his son processed the information, using the edge of the rock to etch lines on the flagstone.

Eventually, Tony turned his head to look at his father. "I guess I get it. You did the same with me, didn't you?"

David nodded.

"For the big picture."

"Yes."

"Okay."

22 DAVID

That evening, Meira lay at his side, picking at the sheet, obviously fretting. He'd told her about their sail and the words he and Tony had exchanged, but she hadn't been there. And later, he'd done his best to engage Tony in basketball before they'd all played gin rummy. Too bad she didn't like basketball. She might be tired enough to sleep if she'd been out there with them.

David leaned over to kiss her nose. "Tony will be okay. We have all summer to help him learn how to be a Jewish boy."

She sniffled. Swiped at her cheek. "Will he ever completely forgive us?"

"I think he already has, at least as much as he'll let himself. And when Yaacov and your parents come, they'll help him discover his roots."

"Is it time to take him to visit Israel?"

"Maybe. We'll ask your mother."

"I'd like to see him with Israeli children, making friends with some of the boy cousins his age. Maybe he could learn to speak Hebrew."

"It's going to be confusing for him."

"Oh, David, should we have said no? For his sake, should we never have involved ourselves in this charade?"

"I don't know how we would have reinvented ourselves on our own. And at least by doing this, we may have helped foil a few plots."

She lifted herself on one elbow. "Should we quit now? Stay here with Tony? Just go back to being *us*?"

He drew his hands behind his head and stared at the ceiling for a moment before looking at her. "I don't think we can quit yet. But I promise you, if our son ever needs us more than Israel does, I will be the first to insist we come home. Nothing is worth more than he—and you—to me."

When she leaned in and buried her face in his neck, he drew her closer. The scent of her, that hint of lemony something in her hair, made him tighten his hold.

"Kiss me, David, and remind me how much you love me."

"I'll always love you."

But he kissed her to show her just how much, first tenderly, then wholeheartedly, until both of them forgot about terrorists and fear as those kisses robbed them of all but sensation.

Later, he held her in his arms and thought how beautiful she was, this not-as-young woman who still made his no-longer-young self taste and feel the magic that was their life together.

FROM FIRE INTO FIRE

The rest of their story—and Tony's—would unfold as it was supposed to. David just had to distract this precious woman when her worry genes tried to take over—and then distract himself as well.

He closed his eyes and shot up a prayer for their boy and his future. David was so grateful for everything. For this wife of his heart. For their son. For the shedding of regrets and the joy of a life lived to the fullest. "Thank you. *Toda*," he whispered, speaking both heavenward and toward the beauty tucked at his chest.

Her breath tickled his skin. "I love you. So very much."

THE END

ACKNOWLEDGMENTS

As always, I'm so blessed to have Jane Lebak and Robin Patchen as critique partners. When I began to write this novella, I thought it would be simple. You know, just a shorter version of a novel. I was delusional. I've never struggled over a story as I did this one. I thought I had a good draft in the fall of 2015. It was short. It got the job done. Jane thought otherwise.

I rewrote. And yet, I'm not William Goldman, and this is not *The Princess Bride*. (Although I could wish…) Still, with Jane's help and Robin's help and then Ray Rhamey's editorial comments, I have this, my attempt to explain how Tony and his parents got into the business.

Along with this brilliant threesome, I want to thank John Pelkey and some of my other Street Team members for their proofreading help and their faithful encouragement when I want to throw up my hands. Hugs and blessings to Susan Walters Peterson, Carol M. Boyer, Amy Campbell, Bonnie K. Tesh, Karen Riley, and DeeJay Sakata.

And also my darling Michael, who reads my fight scenes and keeps me focused.

A Note About What Follows

Meet Tony again in *Two From Isaac's House*—all grown up, and facing his match not only in an international terrorism ring, but in a Southern sailing girl who just happens to be as smart as he is. And should be smart enough not to get involved, but you know how these things are.

Following are the first two chapters of the novel to whet your appetite. If you enjoy either of these—or any of my books—would you be so kind as to leave a review? Authors write with readers in mind—and we like to know if we've succeeded.

From author Normandie Fischer comes a new romantic suspense that takes the reader from the hills of Italy to the Jordanian desert and from there to an Israel on the brink of war with Hamas.

Two from Isaac's House

Rina Lynne has never traveled far from Morehead City, North Carolina. So when she inherits her father's secret stash, she's ready to kick up her heels and go adventuring before she settles down to marry her long-time fiancé. First stop, Italy.

Enter Tony (aka Anton), an engineering geek conned into helping his Israeli cousins as a sort-of spy. From the moment he meets Rina, he's distracted, which is not a good idea when there's already been murder and theft. And from the moment Rina meets Tony, she's fascinated, which is also not a good idea. He's an Arab-American, and she's half-Jewish. And engaged. And then there are all those bodies dropping around them, each linked to the gathering storm in the Middle East.

1 Rina

A moment in time and the rabbit hole opened, tumbling Rina Lynne smack dab into the middle of her own personal wonderland. The voice in her head cried, "Too much, too soon."

She shushed it. This wasn't too much, nor was it too soon. She'd been freed from the need to cower, and this—oh, yes, *this*—was her chance to soar, if only for a season.

A train's whistle ricocheted in the cavernous station, and voices shouted over the hiss of brakes, upping the tension as she compared her ticket to the sign above her head. *Please* let her not be on the wrong track about to board a train that would spit her out in Milan, Frankfurt, or Bucharest—instead of the Umbrian town of Perugia.

Dragging her albatross of a suitcase down the platform, she muttered an under-the-breath word she'd been taught never to say. That luggage salesman had certainly seen this Morehead City girl coming. He'd flashed his oily smile and promised she could carry her world in one rolling, easy-to-handle bag. She should have exchanged it before flying 4600 miles to a country where she didn't speak the language.

A tall man—a very tall man—mounted the steep steps, wearing a backpack and carrying a duffle bag. He glanced down, a definite twinkle in his blue eyes, before he reached back, grasped the handle atop her gargantuan case, and hoisted it up with ease.

"Thank you so much," she said, adding a smile and a *"Grazie."*

He nodded. His "You're welcome" sounded very American. Her own smile lingered as he disappeared into the train and she searched for a seat.

She pictured the glint in those eyes. His height had made her five-foot-ten frame feel petite, and wasn't that a novelty? Jason, at barely five-eleven, never wanted her to wear heels, but sometimes a girl needed fancy to feel feminine.

What if . . . ?

Stop it. There would be no what-ifs.

She wasn't in Italy to find romance because, of course, she'd already found it with Jason. These next months were about seeing something of the world and making memories.

A man seated next to the window of an otherwise empty compartment remained hidden behind his newspaper when she pushed her suitcase through the door. His legs, her legs, and the case took up all the available floor space, but she couldn't heft the thing to the rack above. She drew a paperback from her purse and settled in, determined to ignore him—until his rustling paper recaptured her attention.

He folded it and shifted his gaze to the window as the train accelerated out of town. His cropped black hair and caramel skin, the flat-tipped nose over a shortened upper lip, along with a well-trimmed black mustache made him look like a Mafia goon. And here she sat, alone with him in this small space, although safe, surely, with the door open and her suitcase between them.

When he turned in her direction, his eyes appeared as slits. She ducked her head, but not before she saw the ragged scar that sliced through one eyebrow.

The train clackety-clacked north, its rhythm lulling her toward sleep, but she couldn't doze off alone in a compartment with a man who looked like he'd slipped off the set of *The Godfather*. And, yet, would she be so fearful if he were handsome? Or if he were that American?

Then, just as she was talking herself into compassion for him, he reached over his head to slide a magazine from the pocket of his duffel bag. That innocuous movement opened his jacket to reveal something tan and V-shaped hanging from his shoulder, a leather something with a black handle sticking out the top. She tried to look away, anyplace but at the gun, and shifted her attention to the corridor. When she stole a glance in his direction, the full-faced photograph of a bearded mullah stared back from the middle of exclamatory squiggles. So, not only a gunman, not only a B-grade-movie-type thug, but an Arab (or Iranian?) gunman, probably a terrorist, maybe one of those death-squad bullies. Al Qaeda? Hamas? ISIS?

She concentrated on slowing breaths that would expose her fear. What if he wore one of those bomb things under his shirt? Terrorists hated Americans. They especially hated Jews. She was all of one, half of the other.

Tan and gray towns flashed past the window. Some jumped out of green backgrounds as if plucked complete from a storybook, and others appeared sculpted into the stones. Olive trees patterned the slopes, their leaves glinting silver in the sunlight. And there beside the tracks was the stream-like Tiber, so different from Bogue Sound, the pre-ocean tidal area that separated the North Carolina mainland from the Outer Banks.

Her thoughts fled to the waters of home, to the Sound and the islands fronting it, to her Sunfish and the peace that came when she tucked herself onboard and took off for hours at a time. Like a surfboard zipping over the waves on an ocean breeze, her little boat flew across the water, hampered neither by shoals nor tidal restraints on the way to and from Cape Lookout.

Too bad Jason didn't like to sail, but she'd be back out there someday, Jason or no, her one point of independence in a world that had offered too few chances to rebel.

Before her father's death, her life had been circumscribed and limited to trips to Atlantic Beach or sailing her little Sunfish. Death brings change, but how often does it recalibrate a lens to this extent? Uncovered secrets can dry tears faster than most anything else. Certainly faster than her father's old slap-to-the-cheek method or his cold words, which had begun shortly after her mama's death from cancer all those years ago.

The Arab/Iranian gunman shifted position. He checked his watch, set the magazine on the seat opposite his, and stood. Negotiating past her suitcase and feet, he left the compartment and turned toward the front of the train.

She'd move, find a toilet, go look for another seat. She tucked her book away and gathered her purse. No one would touch her big bag. Still, she whispered, "Stay," as if it were a dog.

SAMPLE TWO FROM ISAAC'S HOUSE

The bathroom wasn't very clean, but the door locked, and the toilet paper dispenser had real, if slightly scratchy, tissue. A papered seat made the accommodations infinitely superior to the hole in the floor she'd met at a non-upgraded-for-tourists *trattoria* yesterday. "Relax. Remember adventure."

Talking aloud to the walls did as much good as sticking out her tongue at the mirror and succeeded only in making her feel ridiculous. But ridiculous was a step up from terrified.

A lot of people carried guns. Not any she knew, aside from the Morehead City police, but people did. Movies were full of men with shoulder holsters, and some were on the side of peaceful, law-abiding, non-interventionist, non-terrorist humanity. She just needed to relax and act naturally. Soon, she would get off the train, and the gunman and she would go in different directions. And she'd never have to see him again.

She jumped when a thud sounded against the bathroom door. Someone was awfully eager—or in need. Suddenly, something slid down the door's length. The red bar above the handle would tell whoever was in the corridor the toilet was occupied. Maybe if she stayed quiet, he, she, it would go away, go try some other restroom.

The door handle jiggled. She called again, trying to remember the Italian words and came up with *"Un momento."* After a long silence, a sharp slap echoed off the metal wall. She flinched back and held her breath. A whoosh, a rumbling, and clanging noises amplified. It sounded as if the outside door of the car had opened, the door for entrance and egress, supposedly shut except when the train was at full stop. Something raked along the floor, bumped, thumped, and a door banged shut. The outside noises stopped. And then—quiet. At least, a relative quiet. The track's rattle still echoed from the drain below the toilet.

The effort to muffle breaths that wanted to whoosh through her lips forced her eyes closed. Someone might still be out there.

At a peremptory knock, she nearly fell off the seat. Words in Italian, a child's voice whined. She croaked out, "*Sì*. Coming," then washed her hands and opened the door.

A smiling woman waited with a small boy. Just an ordinary child with an ordinary need. Rina glanced in both directions before heading back to her suitcase and the safety of the known.

The gunman was back, flipping through his magazine again. She caught her toe under the suitcase and fell forward, landing on the empty space beside him. "I'm sorry, so clumsy of me."

He whipped his gaze in her direction. "Anh."

Was that a word in whatever language he spoke or merely a grunt in answer to her apology? He didn't look confused, so she assumed he understood English.

She tried to smile as she recovered, but her upper lip caught on too-dry teeth. Out the window, the sun still shone, and little wisps of cloud still decorated the sky as the train lumbered toward its destination. She glanced at her watch but didn't register the time as the gunman returned to his magazine. Nothing had happened. Everything was normal. The thump had meant nothing. Neither had the banging.

Breathe in, breathe out, breathe in, breathe out.

Maybe she'd dreamed it all. Maybe the man across from her had toppled out of one of Auntie Luze's romance novels and was really an Arab sheik—no, an outlaw—who carried a ruby-encrusted dagger with which he planned to kidnap and hold her for ransom at his desert outpost. Before she could people the daydream with a hero, two women walked past the compartment. One, tall and red-haired, spoke over her shoulder to the second. "He wasn't in the club car?" Her voice carried the flavor of the South.

The other woman's accent was British. "No, and the train's not that large, is it?"

Two women wandering the corridor, chatting, and a man reading his magazine—each behaving normally. All was well.

It was, as long as the scarred man didn't follow her off the train. As long as she never saw him or his gun again.

2 TONY

Tony Rasad flung the pillow off his head and blinked as the afternoon sun hit his grit-filled eyes. The trip had been grueling: a delayed flight out of Amman, the plane diverted to Athens because of mechanical issues, and then the train that had deposited him here in Perugia. He'd slept the night and half the day away, barely noticing his accommodations. Until now.

The room was incredibly ugly, all purples and blues in a sort of fake splendor. A melancholy as heavy as the room's plum-colored curtains settled, and he wanted it off him, it and the anger at being sucked into a useless operation by a few men who said he could help the cause of peace.

Right. Sure.

He was six-foot-four and wandering among midgets. How did the boys in Jerusalem imagine he'd pass unnoticed in Italy?

He clamped his lips against a curse, but the fault was his.

He'd let his cousin Zif and Zif's friends at Israeli headquarters talk him into this masquerade. He'd bought the tickets. He'd flown to Rome and taken the train to Perugia. No one had hijacked him.

He'd damped his frustration last night with a few glasses of good red wine after the English-speaking barman had tried to dose him with a wretched brandy called Stock 84. One sip later, and he'd slid the snifter across the counter and asked for the best they had in Chiantis, and, no, he didn't care about the cost. The wine had been as smooth as it was soporific.

He climbed from the bed, padded over to the window, and pushed it open. The scent of fresh coffee wafted up from the terrace and, behind it, the perfume of some flower, oleander perhaps. Cups rattled. Muted conversation floated on air with just a hint of chill to it.

His thoughts turned to the long-legged beauty from the train and her struggle to lift that ridiculous suitcase. He liked how tall she was. Tall could stare at his chin instead of his shirt buttons. And her accent spoke of the South, making him want to hear more. Her height and that dark wavy hair of hers—oh, right, and the gray-blue eyes and those lips—how could he not be curious?

Curious also about what had brought her here. He'd seen her flag a taxi as he'd left the station in search of his own transportation. Was she playing tourist? Studying the language? Perugia wasn't the sort of place to attract the traveler in search of adventure, not from what he'd read about it.

So, questions to ask when, if, he encountered her again.

If he dared.

He shouldn't dare. He should keep to his agenda and be done with it.

SAMPLE TWO FROM ISAAC'S HOUSE

But three months was a long time to go without any English conversation. Granted, he might finish in a week or two. Or four.

He'd requested a three-month sabbatical from work to coincide with the length of the course, but it was an unpaid sabbatical. Good thing he had enough in his investment account to tide him over, because the stipend from Israel wouldn't stretch to luxury. And Achmed, the creep, had given him squat.

Except for those orders to find the leak in Achmed's pet student group here in Perugia. A student group that had come under the scrutiny of Tony's Israeli cousin because of Achmed's interest in it. What had Zif said? "If the man sends you to Perugia, he must be using those boys as more than a recruiting arm for Abu Sadiq."

After a little digging, Zif had come back with information from Israeli intelligence sources. "Looks like Abu Sadiq has been using Perugia as a front or even a conduit for terrorist activities in other parts of Europe, including Switzerland and France, a sort of terrorist cell in the making. We've tracked Internet postings and hard-copy letters from Perugia. Now that Achmed's given you an entrée into the group, you can provide eyes on the ground."

Tony wished he'd never heard of Achmed or the man's own personal Palestinian terrorist group, Abu Sadiq. Even the name bothered Tony. Take the Arabic word *abu*, which meant father. That wasn't so bad, but couple father with the name *Sadiq*, which meant any number of things in English, including truth and virtuous, and he thought he'd puke. The idea of killers puffing out their chest because they were sons of truth and virtue—or fathers of it, depending on how you looked at the name—sickened him.

Why had he agreed to any of this? Playing double agent had felt wrong from the beginning. Of course it had, with "playing" the operative word. Playacting the terrorist sympathizer, playacting the Israeli informant.

Well, no, he didn't suppose he really played at the second. But the first?

Of course, Achmed would have shot him on the spot if he'd said, *"Lá shukran*, no thank you, not interested."

No, his problem stemmed from having agreed to infiltrate Abu Sadiq on even the most casual basis. Now everyone had claws in him.

His stomach growled, reminding him that his last food had been consumed hours ago. He didn't want caffeine in his system, which might get in the way of the sleep he'd like to return to as soon as possible. Better a cool beer and a sandwich. He dialed room service.

"Pronto."

"Hello, I mean, *ciao.*"

"Yes, sir?"

"Oh, you speak English? You don't know how happy that makes me. I'd like to order a *birra*—make that two of your best. I don't know, maybe a pale ale?"

The man mentioned brands that meant nothing to him, but he agreed to one and asked also for a prosciutto and mozzarella sandwich.

"And if the waiter can just set the tray inside, a tip will be on the table."

"Subito, signore. Right away."

He filled the claw-footed tub in the bathroom with steaming water and let the heat work on his tense muscles.

When he heard the door click shut behind the waiter, he dripped over to the food and carried it back to the bathroom. Two bottles of beer, a sandwich, and a hot bath. What more could he want?

Peace, perhaps. A trip home to the lake cottage in New York State where spring blooms would be bursting forth. His mother had planted dozens of perennials that took care of themselves. And his little sailboat was stored there. Or how about a week on the beach in Tel Aviv, sailing on the Med? Yeah, he could think of a lot of things he'd rather be doing.

Although he was shedding fatigue and, with it, some of the hostility he'd been hoarding since his last interview with Achmed, enough stuck to make him want to tell Achmed and Bahir, along with his cousin Zif's crew, just where they could all go.

He was an American. With Israeli cousins. A man who didn't belong anywhere near a terrorist camp. He remembered how excited his childhood friend, Bahir, had been when he'd discovered the job offer Tony'd received in Amman. "Tony, you can help the cause! Be one of us!"

It killed him to think about Bahir. To remember that long-ago innocence when they'd dashed from one house to the other and played on the beach near Beirut, thinking they were brothers. Thinking they were the same. In the days of their childhood, neither he nor Bahir had known the truth.

They weren't brothers. They'd never been and never would be.

When Achmed and Bahir discovered his lies? Heaven help him. And uncover the truth they would. He was a lousy actor. Most days, he felt like a bumbling fool.

He should have told Bahir the truth back when they were

boys, right after he'd learned it from his parents. But that would have meant betraying them. So he'd kept his lips zipped and let Bahir believe that he, too, stood on the Palestinian side of the fence.

And then good old cousin Zif at Israeli headquarters had suggested Tony help the homeland by putting his ears to the ground at the Abu Sadiq camp. No field work. Just a little transfer of information back and forth.

So, here he was, pretending to help his boyhood friend Bahir and Bahir's boss by passing on information he gleaned when he traveled from Amman to Ashkelon or Haifa as an engineer for the Scarborough Oil Company—because, hey, he was an American and could move about freely in Israel. Who would question him?

Tony took another long swig of beer, then closed his eyes and lay back in the warm water, his head resting against the tile. The beer did nothing to ease what his thoughts churned up. Achmed's ugly face loomed behind his closed lids.

According to Achmed, too many details known only to the movement's elite had filtered out of bounds into international intelligence circles. They weren't big secrets. Nobody in the field had access to the big secrets, but when a supposedly private memorandum wended its way from someplace in Italy through England and into the hands of a sympathetic Frenchman, Achmed's profanities had ended in him deputing Tony to Perugia. "You have traveled much. You will blend in."

Again that assumption that Tony could possibly go unnoticed.

Achmed's thick lips had spread over stained and uneven teeth as he offered Tony a glass of hot, sugared tea. They'd been at the training camp just south of Amman, in the largest of the cinderblock buildings that provided housing and offices for the group's elite. Recruits slept in tents. And all around was dirt and dust and heat.

"No one will imagine that you come as anything other than my envoy," Achmed had said in an offhand manner that belied the gleam in his heavy-lidded eyes. "In a friendly sort of way, an American studying the language. So, you add a new one to your repertoire. How many will that make?"

Tony'd kept his hands at his side, flexing his fingers so they wouldn't ball into fists. Just being in the same room with the man made him want to slug something. Preferably the guy's face. "Five."

"You see, it is an altogether profitable thing for you to go. And you will find the one who is so careless with my words. You will be able to leave your job for this time?"

"Presumably. But couldn't I be more useful interpreting things out of Israel?"

Achmed's smile had vanished as he snapped a pencil point against his thumb, and his eyes had narrowed. "Perhaps you are correct. Still, I doubt there will be a war this month, and you will go. Bahir has all the details for you. Including your tickets."

Shaking off the memory—because he hadn't a clue about any of it and was really foundering here—he climbed from the tub, dried off, and picked up his razor. He hated having left things unsettled between him and Bahir. And probably hated it more because of the constant nagging guilt. If Bahir even imagined the truth… No, he wouldn't go there. All he got from thinking like that was a migraine.

He wanted this thing started and finished. He would do what he had to and be as sneaky as possible and tell all the lies required of him. Then, as soon as he could, he'd hightail it back to Jordan and double his efforts to convince Bahir he didn't belong among the scorpions of Abu Sadiq. It was past time for Bahir to quit playing number two man to Achmed the Scumbag Terrorist.

Perhaps if he could uncover the truth about the murder of Bahir's parents and lay that truth at his friend's feet, it might help. He was certain it hadn't been Israel behind the Lebanese car bombing, in spite of what Achmed claimed.

He finished his second beer before making the phone call to Yusuf, his first step in the business that had brought him here. Yeah, and wasn't he looking forward to getting to know the local boys?

But if he didn't, how would he figure out who worked for whom and why?

Yusuf answered on the third ring, responding to Tony's introduction with "Now? Excellent. You cannot miss me. I am short and round, and my hair, it continues to retreat."

"I can—"

"And you are tall, yes? I have heard that. I will await you at the Bar Turreno, you know that one? Near the fountain? I will be reading . . . I think a newspaper, *l'Unità*."

The bar was darkly paneled, though light spilled through the front windows. Tony paused in the doorway, followed the waving hand, and slid onto the bench across from the balding Yusuf, who folded his paper and smiled. "Anton? Anton Rasad? Yusuf Ajani. *Marhaba*."

Tony answered the Arabic hello and said, "Call me Tony."

"*Kaif al-hal?* How are you after your travels?"

"Much better since I've had a little sleep."

"That is a terrible trip to do all at once. Myself, I prefer to stay over a night or two in Rome. Still, you are here, and I welcome you."

"*Shukran.* Thank you."

"Coffee? Something?"

Tony shook his head. "I ate."

"Well, I have found a room for you. If it meets your requirements, you may move in this evening or tomorrow morning. The signora is very accommodating. Also, there is Internet."

"Excellent. The hotel is fine, but I'd like to unpack and get settled."

"I must tell you," Yusuf said, with a sheepish grin, "there is a daughter, but the view makes up for her."

"Good thing I don't plan to be here long enough to worry about a woman or her mama."

The other man laughed. Tony couldn't help responding to such good humor.

"I will take you to see it after I introduce you to some of the recruits."

They stood, and Yusuf reached behind Tony to usher him from the café. Only, the touch didn't exactly land on his lower back.

That height issue again. His butt was not a place he wanted another man's hands. His dad, he hugged. His uncles. Even some of his cousins. But guy friends? Other than the one-armed, quick-let's-barely-touch hug? Thanks, but no thanks, even if he had grown up in a touchy-feely Arab culture.

"This way," Yusuf said, oblivious to that personal-space intrusion. "Some new students have joined us recently, including an older man I have yet to meet. Ibrahim Hawaat was to come on the same train as you. He will study at the university, medicine they say, and will work with us." A pause as he led them around a corner to a narrower street, and then, "There was trouble on that train of yours. Do you know anything about it?"

"Trouble? What sort?" Tony had been too exhausted to notice much of anything.

Not that it mattered.

"An Englishman, Mr. Andrew Darling, has disappeared. He traveled with my fiancée, Natalie, and the police, they are considering that perhaps he left the train unwillingly."

"You mean was pushed off?" That got his attention. So much for it not mattering. Murder, if that's what this was, always mattered. And an Englishman with ties through this Natalie to the head of the Abu Sadiq base in Italy? Achmed had mentioned the stolen memorandum having passed through English hands.

"They do not know yet. I think perhaps they doubted Natalie when she first inquired and did not want to consider that such a thing could happen on their railroad, certainly not without someone noticing. Natalie wished to show her friend Perugia. We were to spend today with him."

"That's too bad."

"It is. Natalie is furious that no one does anything. This helps her, the anger. She has returned to Terni, because she is a teacher of English, but she has promised to come this weekend. Perhaps you can meet her."

"I would like that. And let me know if you discover more about the Englishman. As you said, I was on that train."

After sipping tea with some of the students and handing

over a month's rent for the room with a view, Tony headed back to his hotel. He was itching to report what he'd learned about a missing Englishman with ties to the group here.

He booted up his computer, inserted the security device into a USB port, and signed on to the Internet with the secure connection his cousin had provided. Then he began to type.

End of Sample.

About the Author

I invite you to visit my website to learn more about my passions—sailing, family, good books, and good food—and to sign up to hear about new releases in e-book, print, and audio. I also give away the occasional goodies to subscribers.

Connect with me. I'd love to hear from you.
www.normandiefischer.com
www.facebook/NormandieFischer
@WritingOnBoard

Also by Normandie Fischer
WOMEN'S FICTION

BECALMED
2014 Heart of Excellence finalist

When a Southern woman with a broken heart finds herself falling for a widower with a broken boat, it's anything but smooth sailing.

With her days chock full - designing jewelry for the shop she co-owns with her best friend, sailing her sharpie, and hanging out with girlfriends—Tadie Longworth barely notices she's morphing into the town's maiden aunt. When Will, a widower with a perky daughter named Jilly, limps into town in a sailboat badly in need of engine repairs, Tadie welcomes the chance to help. Her shop becomes Jilly's haven while Will hunts boat parts, and Tadie even takes the two of them sailing. It's the kind of thing she lives for, and it's a welcome distraction from the fact that her ex-boyfriend Alex, aka The Jerk of Jerks, is back in town. With his northern bride. Oh, and he's hitting on Tadie, too.

Those entanglements are more than enough, thank you very much, so it's almost a relief when a hurricane blows into town: at least the weather can match Tadie's mood. When Will and Jilly take shelter in her home, though, Tadie finds herself battling her attraction to Will. Even worse, the feeling is mutual, tempting them all with what-ifs that petrify Will, who has sworn never to fall in love again. Mired in misunderstanding, he takes advantage of the clear skies and hauls Jilly out of there and back to his broken boat so fast, Tadie's head spins.

With the man she might have loved gone, and the man she wishes gone showing up on her doorstep, Tadie finds herself like a sailboat with no wind; becalmed, she has to fight her way back against the currents to the shores of the life, and the man, she wants.

HEAVY WEATHER
2016 Award of Excellence Finalist

It takes a town to save a child. That town is Beaufort, North Carolina.

Annie Mac's estranged husband vows that nothing will stop him from getting his baby girl. Not Annie Mac and certainly not that boy of hers.

Only four blocks away, Hannah Morgan lives in comfort with her husband and dog, making pottery and waiting for her best friend to come home. When she discovers the two children cowering in the bushes and their mama left for dead, it doesn't take her long to set her coterie of do-gooders to some extra-strength do-gooding. Add in Clay, a lonely police lieutenant yanked out of his comfort zone and into the heart of this small family, and who knows what will happen?

From the author of *Becalmed* comes this latest tale of the Carolina coast, introducing some new characters to love—and to loathe.

SAILING OUT OF DARKNESS
2014 Aspen Gold Finalist
2014 Maggie Award Finalist
2014 Selah Award Finalist

Love conquers all?
Maybe for some people.

When Samantha flies to Italy to gain distance from a disastrous affair with her childhood best friend, the last thing on her mind is romance. But Teo Anderson is nothing like her philandering ex-husband or her sailing buddy, Jack, who, despite his live-in girlfriend, caught her off guard with his flashing black eyes.

Teo has his own scars, both physical and emotional, that

he represses by writing mysteries—until one strange and compelling vision comes to life in the person of Sam. Seeking answers, he offers friendship to this obviously hurting woman, a friendship that threatens to upend his fragile peace of mind.

But not even sailing the cobalt waters of the Mediterranean can assuage Sam's guilt for destroying Jack's relationship and hurting another woman. Soon the consequences of her behavior escalate, and the fallout threatens them all.

Sailing out of Darkness is the haunting story of mistakes and loss ... and the grace that abounds through forgiveness.

Made in the USA
Columbia, SC
24 April 2023